TAKING OFF THE WRAPS

Skye Fargo couldn't believe this was the same Bridget Delahay who had looked so prim and proper in her high-necked dress, and whose lips were pursed with disapproval when she met him.

Her dress was off now, along with her boots and petticoats and string-tied lacy drawers. What was left was the most un-prim and improper vision that a man could want to see.

Her lips were relaxed now, as she sighed in delicious contentment after Skye's easy-to-take lesson in loving.

"I think I have misspent my youth," she said. "I will have to make arrangements so I can make up for lost time."

Fargo stretched back on the bedroll and grinned up at her. "Give me a few minutes, and I'll rearrange you. It's gonna be a long night," Fargo whispered. . . .

⊘ SIGNET WESTERNS BY JON SHARPE

(0451)

RIDE THE WILD TRAIL

THE TRAILSMAN 58

SLAUGHTER
EXPRESS

by

Jon Sharpe

Ⓢ
A SIGNET BOOK

NEW AMERICAN LIBRARY

NAL BOOKS ARE AVAILABLE AT QUANTITY DISCOUNTS
WHEN USED TO PROMOTE PRODUCTS OR SERVICES.
FOR INFORMATION PLEASE WRITE TO PREMIUM MARKETING DIVISION,
NEW AMERICAN LIBRARY, 1633 BROADWAY,
NEW YORK, NEW YORK 10019.

The first chapter of this book previously appeared in *Fortune Riders*, the fifty-seventh volume in this series.

SIGNET TRADEMARK REG. U.S. PAT. OFF. AND FOREIGN COUNTRIES
REGISTERED TRADEMARK—MARCA REGISTRADA
HECHO EN CHICAGO, U.S.A.

SIGNET, SIGNET CLASSIC, MENTOR, ONYX, PLUME, MERIDIAN
and NAL BOOKS are published by New American Library,
1633 Broadway, New York, New York 10019

First Printing, October, 1986

1 2 3 4 5 6 7 8 9

PRINTED IN THE UNITED STATES OF AMERICA

The Trailsman

Beginnings . . . they bend the tree and they mark the man. Skye Fargo was born when he was eighteen. Terror was his midwife, vengeance his first cry. Killing spawned Skye Fargo, ruthless, cold-blooded murder. Out of the acrid smoke of gunpowder still hanging in the air, he rose, cried out a promise never forgotten.

The Trailsman, they began to call him, all across the West: searcher, scout, hunter, the man who could see where others only looked, his skills for hire but not his soul, the man who lived each day to the fullest, yet trailed each tomorrow. Skye Fargo, the Trailsman, the seeker who could take the wildness of a land and the wanting of a woman and make them his own.

Indian Summer, 1861—
just before an effort to open the Bozeman Trail
from Fort Laramie to the Montana goldfields
brought open war in northern Wyoming

1

The dust was six inches thick on Post Street in Fort Laramie, and a man was having his face ground into it. Skye Fargo could hear him grunt in pain as his attacker lifted a heavy boot and thumped it repeatedly into his belly and ribs.

Initially, two others had helped pull the slender, sallow-skinned man off his horse and batter him into the dust. Fargo had glimpsed this gang-up as he came downstairs from the hotel above the Rounders Saloon, and had watched it from the hole-in-the-wall entrance, squinting irritably, while he grew accustomed to the midmorning sunlight. He'd been on his way to the barber's for a bath and trim, a big, tousled man in a buckskin jacket, feeling scruffy and knowing he looked it. His pale-blue eyes were slightly bloodshot, his black-bearded face a little puffed, for he'd just left the bed and booze of a sweet-juicin' waitress.

Right now, though, he felt just enough twist to interfere with the unfair fight. He wedged through the gathering crowd. By the time he broke to the front, the two attackers had desisted, their victim on his knees, leaving the finishing touches to a red-haird, red-whiskered bruiser in a frock coat who, by the smirk on his thick lips, was enjoying his task.

There was something vaguely familiar about the redhead that made Fargo take a sharper look. He smiled then, coldly, recognizing that fat mouth and piggish eyes. Along much of the Oregon Trail, Tully Nickles had a mean reputation with a gun—and indeed, Fargo saw Nickles' hickory-handled Colt Navy protruding from the holster low on his thigh, rigged for a quick draw. From the trail's beginning at Independence, Missouri, westward past Fort Laramie to South Pass in the Rockies, there was a saying that Nickles' revolver went to the highest bidder—and he'd always been busy.

"Git up, you yaller dawg," Nickles growled. "You've been paradin' around here like you're a man, so c'mon and prove it."

Fargo glimpsed the slight bulge underneath the sallow man's coat on the left side, indicating a concealed armpit holster. The man was armed, probably with a stubby-barreled .36- or .38-caliber storekeeper's model pistol, but it wouldn't do him any good. By the time he got his hand inside his coat, he'd be a dead man. It was a mystery to Fargo why somebody wanted the man out of the way, but it was clear Tully Nickles had been selected for the job.

"Yuh ain't got a hair on your ass if you—" Nickles began. He didn't finish the sentence, his victim finally goaded by pain and embarrassment into making his fatal move. One of the gawking bystanders yelled in alarm as the man fumbled to draw, and Nickles' right hand swept to the hickory butt of his revolver.

As the Colt slid from the well-oiled holster, Skye Fargo thrust through the crowd in a flying dive. Powerful fingers gripped Nickles' wrist, forcing the weapon away from the man. It discharged with a blast, and now other onlookers shouted, this time more in fear. Fargo grinned over Nickles' shoulder, never relaxing his grip. He wrapped his left arm around Nickles' head, forearm pressed against the gunman's throat, tightening his pressure. Nickles dropped his revolver to the dust, and Fargo kicked it away with his boot, then caught him by the left arm, spun him around, and smashed a heavy fist into Nickles' gaping face.

Nickles stumbled backward into the crowd. Blood trickled from his split lips as he reeled, recognition coming into his dazed eyes.

"Remember me?" Fargo asked coolly.

"Skye Fargo! Damned right I do, you bastard."

Fargo grinned. He handed his high-crowned hat to the nearest spectator and then slipped out of his jacket. He stood out in the center of the circle, a lean and feral glint to his eyes. "Come again?"

"Comin' plenty." Nickles grunted, plunging forward, huge fists balled and hairy, hatred written across his broad face.

Fargo waited for him, eyes shifting to the two men who had been in the fight at the beginning. He glimpsed the beaten man crawl to the edge of the circle, shaking his head groggily; then his view was consumed by Tully Nickles lashing out with his right fist and trying to drive Fargo to the ground. Fargo ducked and again his hard-knuckled hand snapped out, this time catching Nickles in the bridge of the nose and breaking it cleanly. Gore gushed out as Nickles tottered onward, screaming with pain. His two *compadres* had shifted positions and were coming up on either side of Fargo, the smaller of the pair—a stocky, balding man in dirty garb—diving toward Fargo's knees.

"Tackle 'im, Grady," the other gent yelled.

Fargo danced back lightly and then brought his right foot up with all the force he could muster. The toe of his boot dug into Grady's stomach, knocking the wind from his lungs. He gasped once and then lay on his face shivering, digging stubby fingers into the dust, vomiting his last meal in a puddle under his face.

Nickles was up and full of fight despite his broken nose. Tears coursed down his cheeks as he lunged in again, while the third man, a rangy chap in tan shirt and flat-crowned teamster's hat, rushed in from the other side. Skye Fargo dodged in between the two of them as the crowd yelled in appreciation. Pivoting suddenly, Fargo charged the third man, hitting him half a dozen times in the face with fierce, lightninglike punches before stepping away to meet Nickles again.

Somewhere, somehow, Nickles had come up with a length of iron chain in his hand. Feinting as though to retreat, Fargo caused the gunman to overextend his swing and slipped inside its arc, ramming a fist into Nickles' unguarded belly, doubling him up. He then grabbed hold of the abruptly slackening chain, wrenched Nickles forward, and kneed him solidly in the balls. Nickles turned pale white, pawed at his crotch, and went down in a writhing heap, cursing shrilly.

Fargo tossed the chain aside and stepped back, looking at his bleeding knuckles. Nickles squirmed in the dirt, color slowly returning to his face, eyes glittering with hate. He glanced at his long-barreled revolver lying on the ground a half-dozen yards away.

"Go on, pick it up," Fargo said softly. He shifted his holster so that his Colt was positioned just so. "Go ahead, Tully."

Nickles rubbed his face with the palm of his hand. "I reckon you're gettin' into somethin' bigger than you figured," he croaked. "This wasn't your shindig, Fargo."

"I made it mine. Pick up your gun, if you got the guts."

" 'Nuther time," Nickles growled. He staggered to his feet, wavering, and shifted his glare from Fargo to the beaten man, menace heavy in his voice. "We ain't done either, Jeppson, you'n me."

The man he'd called Jeppson stood purse-lipped, mopping his face with a linen hand-kerchief. His features were a little pale beneath his sallow complexion, but he was unafraid. "Another time, anytime."

Fargo, chuckling derisively, scooped up the dropped revolver, and while Nickles was rousting his two pals, he shucked out the percussion caps and tossed the useless weapon to its owner. Nickles shoved it in his holster and, cupping his groin with one hand and his nose with the other, hastily barged through the crowd, sided by his wobble-legged buddies, in an ignominious retreat to the saloon.

"Thanks," Jeppson said to Fargo.

"My pleasure. Never had much use for Nickles."

"Still, he's right, it wasn't your scrap. You don't know me."

"I know him and I've seen him work before. That's why I stepped in. Hate to say it, mister, but somebody wants you killed."

Jeppson shook his head. "Naw, him an' his pards were just a li'le drunk, is all, and feeling wringy." He was lying and Fargo knew it, although not why. Fargo didn't ask, simply shaking hands as the man introduced himself: "Mel Jeppson, commissary for Regina Express, Mr.—Fargo, did I hear? Yes? Glad to meet you."

"Call me Skye," Fargo replied affably, turning to retrieve his jacket and hat. The big, rawboned bystander who'd held them during the fight was grinning widely; so were the other spectators as they began dispersing, noisily babbling queries and opinions.

Jeppson regarded Fargo as if deliberating, gauging the two-hundred-plus pounds of muscular frame and judging the character of the man within. Abruptly he asked, "You're not from around here, are you?"

"Nope. Just hit town yesterday, in from Nebraska way."

"Looking for work?"

"With John Bozeman, I am, but I haven't found him."

"Christ, you like living risky, don't you? Well, the latest scuttlebutt is that Bozeman's been delayed by lack of money or official permission or some such, and won't get here for a few months."

"Damn! I might've guessed." Annoyed, Fargo brushed back the wave of black hair that habitually fell over half his forehead, and snugged his hat down tight. "Okay, I could use a job."

"C'mon, then, I'll take you to Regina."

The bystander interrupted with a sardonic laugh. "F'get it. You got better odds of stayin' alive by trail-blazin' with Bozeman. You're a stranger, else you'd know Luther Chadwick sent out word he don't cotton to Regina, and there ain't a gent in Fort Laramie fool enough to buck him and hire on. Worse luck, them's were a couple of his Consolidated mule skinners. Chadwick won't cotton to you whumpin' 'em, extra more so 'cause it saved Mel and that's a boost for Regina."

Fargo wasn't particularly surprised, for he was well aware of Consolidated and Luther Chadwick. Consolidated Transport ran the largest freight network in the territory, having hundreds of skilled teamsters, prime oxen and mules, the best Murphys and newest Studebaker wagons. Owner Chadwick bossed his vast operation with an iron fist, expanding roughshod, relentlessly busting or absorbing all competition.

All except Regina. Somehow it'd managed to survive, though from the snatches of saloon gossip Fargo had overheard the previous night, Regina Express was a shoestring outfit barely holding on. It hauled just enough cargo to keep its delapidated yard open, cover the feed bill of its crowbait teams, and meet the wages of what few loyal skinners would still whip for it.

And pay, Fargo thought, Mel Jeppson's salary

as commissary in charge of loading and supplying—and of recruiting unwary strangers by explaining little and admitting less. No wonder he fibbed! Even discounting for barroom bullshit, Regina sounded like it was in a helluva tight box, one just about the size of a coffin.

Jeppson's jaw thrust out. "Who asked you to butt in, Hoyte?"

"Now, don't get feisty, Mel," the big man cautioned with a tolerant grin. "Puttin' up a front is fine, but hell, you gotta have somethin' to back it. Instead, you had that fire in your yard, you lost your last two trains, half your crew's quit, and you ain't got no wagon masters. Everyone knows Regina's about to pack it in."

"Everyone's wrong. We are not folding," Jeppson insisted, appealing to Fargo. "See for yourself. We're getting wagons ready for another run, and need teamsters, blacksmiths, wheelwrights—"

"And a wagon master."

"You can handle a full string?"

"Have before, up to a forty-rig bull outfit." Fargo shrugged. "Yeah, I'll go see. Why not? I've got nothing better to do right now."

Hoyte shook his head. "Why not? Chadwick is why not."

"I'll take my chances," Fargo replied, the blue of his eyes darkening a shade. "And Chadwick will have to take his . . ."

Jeppson led Fargo down the street to the edge of town. They crossed the fort road, skipping between two Espenshied model Murphys rumbling toward the Consolidated yards, and headed for the office of Regina Express. It was a long shedlike building of unpainted wood, one story high with a false front. A runway on its left led into Regina's wagonyard, and as Fargo approached the office entrance with Jeppson, they passed the open gates and he got a look at the yard: a large open space, crisscrossed with wheel ruts, and a pair of sagging, hip-roof barns with a hay rack in between them. There were also the charred remains of some sheds, which reminded Fargo of the yard fire Hoyte had mentioned.

Along one side of the yard were eight big freighters. They were ancient wagons, huge clumsy Conestogas of Santa Fe Trail vintage, swagger boxes split and paint-peeled, canvas tilts patched and sagging between the hoops. Their teams were no better—spavined, stove-up mules standing resignedly in a fenced pasture adjacent the barns. A few men sauntered around or sat in the shade of a smithy's forge, where a burly guy in a tattered checked shirt was pounding halfheartedly at a tire rim. He cast a surly glance at Fargo and Jeppson and made a comment that raised a laugh from the men around them.

As they stopped by the office door, Jeppson read the expression on Fargo's face. "Yeah, that's what we've been fighting Consolidated with," he said ruefully, opening the door and ushering Fargo inside.

The office had the usual clutter of file cabinets, bookshelves, stacks of papers and folders, along with an old iron safe in one corner, a moose head on the rear wall, and two large flat-topped desks next to the windows. At the nearer desk sat a young woman. She was in her mid to late twenties, Fargo estimated, and had a cameo face, pert-nosed and green-eyed, and great looping coils of lustrous chestnut hair. She pressed her plump lips, though, into a discouragingly prim smile, looking quite modest in a full-length wrapper of dusty-rose percale.

Politely Jeppson asked, "Bridget, where's Mr. Delahay?"

"He went 'round back to check on some broken hames."

"I'll find him. Mr. Fargo here is maybe interested in a job," Jeppson said, turning to go outside. "Now, you just stay put, Skye."

As the door shut, Bridget murmured, "Oh, really. Skye Fargo." She looked at him, at his clothes, her lips slightly curling in disdain, and then she ignored him.

Fargo began to burn. When she got up to fetch a ledger, he saw she was taller than he'd thought, with ripe breasts and bottom. Her undulating strut made him doubt she could be as uptight proper as she was acting.

The door opened, and a stout, bald man in shirt sleeves and rumpled brown trousers limped inside, leaning on a cane. "Justin Delahay, Mist' Fargo," he announced, poking the door closed with his cane. He stumped to the empty desk, the heartiness of his smile and voice unable to mask the lines of worry creasing his face. "Your name's familiar, dagnabit, I've been tryin' to rec'lect where. P'raps last year, that Fort Caulder ruckus?"

"Could be. I was thereabouts then, and it got kind of busy."

"Busy! Gold, slavers, rampagin' Kiowas ... I followed it close in the army weeklies, account of the wagon train killin's," Delahay explained, easing into his desk chair. "I heard of you from other times, too, I'm sure I have. If you're thinkin' to tie on here as m' master, I imagine you'll do. No question you got the experience."

Bridget sniped, "I should rather say 'experiences.'"

Delahay frowned at her. "M' daughter takes after her mother, God rest her soul," he confided to Fargo, pursing his lips, and then remarked, "Mel told me John Bozeman is what brung you to Fort Laramie."

"The news did, that he was gearing to blaze a trail up to the Montana gold fields and could use another scout. It sounded interesting, and I'd had good dealings with John before, so I came."

"You'd be striking through treaty lands, y'know, like the Sioux hunting grounds east o' the Big Horns. Be crazy dangerous to try."

"I heard working for Regina is just as loco."

"You had a taste of it, too, accordin' to Mel. Much obliged." Delahay drummed fingers on the desk. "It's been bad. Bad going to worse, since I won the gov'ment contract to haul supplies to the Crow River region, for that new army camp and surroundin' settlements."

Fargo nodded, aware of the campsite. It'd been a private fur trade post that the army recently bought and planned to garrison, in preparation for the coming Union Pacific Railroad through there.

"Chadwick wanted that contract, and's still aiming to get it," Delahay continued. "Our last two loads never made it. If our next one fails to arrive, the contract will be canceled. I've already received word from Colonel Garabedian, in command."

"What happened to the two trains?"

"One got lost below Horse Creek. Wound up far afield, stranded when the stock stampeded. Most o' the teamsters deserted. The wagon master, Shorty Rawls, got his neck broken in an accident." Delahay paused. "That beats Abe McHugh, who handled the outfit after Rawls. Abe was scalped three days before they reached the army outpost."

"The second was attacked by Sioux?"

"So I've been told," Delahay replied cynically. "And if the Sioux don't getcha, there's a cholera epidemic that will—or so my men've been told. Scared some away, them's that hadn't gone already from bein' threatened and beaten. Hell, a few were even bought off."

"You have a crew for this next run?"

"There're about thirty men—teamsters, wheel-wrights, stockmen—left with me. They'll stick till Regina goes under." Delahay chuckled a little grimly. "That's probably 'cause no place else would have 'em as crew. Well? Would wagon-masterin' here be too big a challenge?"

"What're you offering, the standard wage?"

"Sure. But I can't afford to pay it all up front. I'll pay what I can now, and the balance when I get paid, after you deliver."

Fargo shook his head. "You can't expect me to take on the risks of the job, plus take a bet on your chances too, just for a few bucks."

"I had a hope, but ... I can't blame you for refusin'."

"No, I'm saying that like every gamble, the more at risk, the more to win. I'll accept—for fifteen percent of any profits from this run."

"Ouch! That's steep." Delahay rubbed his ear.

"Still, not unheard of, and I guess if you're good enough to scout for Bozeman, we won't find you losing yourself breaking trail, like Rawls did."

"No, he's liable to lose himself in the first tavern or brothel." Bridget rose from her chair now and leaned across her desk, her breasts jiggling, swelling with indignation. "Look how he's shown up, still reeking of rotgut and floozies, in need of work but not above trying to gouge us. Oh, you have some nerve, *Mister* Fargo."

"And you've got some mouth," Fargo snapped, moving abruptly, two hands striking the flat of her desk with a bang. "You've got it ass backward to boot. I don't need the work. Regina needs a wagon master. There's not a freighting line in the country that needs one as badly, or a lady who needs a muzzle as badly as you, *Miss* Bridget."

Bridget sat down. "Well! I never—"

"May be your trouble." Fargo grinned, pivoted around, thumbs hooked in his shell belt, and looked calmly at Delahay. "What's your decision?"

Delahay blinked. He looked at his outraged daughter and then at Fargo again, admiration in his eyes. "Damn you." He grinned. "Step out back and get acquainted with crew, and if you're still willin' to run the train afterward, you've got a deal."

Fargo nodded. "When will the next outfit be ready to roll?"

"Soon's tomorrow dawn, if we hustle," Delahay explained. "Sixteen wagons are at the fort quartermaster's, loading seventy-five ton of foodstuffs and sundries. Then there're civilian supplies to take on here, including some heavy mining gear—

hydraulic tools, pumps, new drills." Delahay stuck out his hand. "Good luck meeting the men."

Fargo smiled. Getting acquainted with his teamsters meant only one thing. The tough mule skinners and bull whackers always resented a new wagon master signing up with a company; they'd show their ill will until they believed that the new master could handle himself.

He left the office, giving Bridget a wink as he strolled by. She glared, eyes dark and bitter. He went around into the yard and located Mel Jeppson standing near the front gates, a green eyeshade stuck to his forehead, a pencil in his hand.

"How'd it go, Skye? Get the job?"

Fargo nodded, surveying the yard. He saw that the group of men over by the smithy's was now squatting in a semicircle, some holding dirty playing cards in their hands, while the others watched the game. More men were working around the wagon sheds; others were in a second stock pen farther up along the yard. They were a mixed lot, with a sprinkling of Frenchmen, a few breeds, and one bull-necked giant who must have weighed two-fifty, and very little of it fat. They were ugly and dirty and swamper-mean—the dregs.

"They aren't any more like mule skinners than a pack of coyotes would be," Fargo commented. "Are any of them able to snap a whip?"

"Yeah, quite a few, and Henri the Canuck is real skilled with the blacksnake." Jeppson pointed to a card player, a pock-faced rogue in greasy elk hides. "Okay, they're not the best. We can't hire a decent crew, what with Consolidated pressuring, and lately the rumors of Indians and cholera. And it hasn't been any picnic keeping them sober and more'r less straight. Listen, they'll probably try putting Tiny Quinelle onto you, and I don't advise letting him greet you."

"Tiny's the big one, I bet," Fargo said quietly. "It figures. All right, Mel, tell them. And then stay back out of the way."

Jeppson called, "Boys—meet the new wagon master, Skye Fargo."

Nonchalantly, Fargo lit a thin panatella cigar and sauntered toward the smithy's. Men began converging from the sheds and pens, but the card players remained seated on the ground, barely paying him any notice as he came up and stopped in front of their circle.

"Well, boys," Fargo said easily, "let's get to work."

A mulatto grinned, revealing a row of pearly teeth. Henri the Canuck laughed in a high-pitched voice, and the burly man who had been laboring with the tire rim looked up, sweat beading his face.

Fargo smiled. "One of you boys help the gentleman with the wheel. You others can start greasing axles."

"We don't use them wagons, boss," another player said—a scarred man packing four Green River knives. "The wagons are all over at Fort La-rummy's depot."

Fargo nodded. He was standing just above the large man, Tiny Quinelle, who had a huge head of kinky brown hair and a sleeveless shirt revealing tremendous arms. "We'd like to keep the other wagons in condition. We may be using them

23

shortly," he explained pleasantly. He glanced at Jeppson, spotted Delahay and Bridget watching from the office windows, and then turned back, features hardening. "Move your lazy butts," he snapped, and pointed a finger directly at the giant. "And you, Tiny. You go saddle me a horse."

His order hit them by surprise, for they hadn't expected him to deliberately pick on Quinelle. Quinelle looked Fargo over from head to foot and then spat on his boot. The mulatto went into hysterical guffaws. Fargo, tightening his teeth on the cigar, abruptly bent down and grasped Quinelle by his shirt front, yanking him to his feet. His right fist shot up, catching Quinelle flush on the jaw and knocking him against the wall of the shed.

Fargo heard Mel Jeppson shout, and then he leapt through the circle of startled men, knocking cards and money aside. Quinelle was trying to straighten himself out, but Henri the Canuck was scrambling up, his blacksnake whip in his hand. Fargo pivoted on one foot and kicked out with the other, his spat-upon boot catching Henri in the stomach while the Canuck was lifting the stock of his whip. As Henri doubled over, Fargo stepped in with a short uppercut to the chin. There was no more fight in the French-Canadian.

But there was plenty of fight left in Quinelle. He charged Fargo with his arms wide open. Instead of meeting Quinelle directly, Fargo sidestepped at the last instant, figuring the man would thunder past him, but Quinelle was surprisingly quick for his size, and turned, forcing Fargo back. Fargo retreated, delivering swift, short-range knucklers to solar plexus and gut, and a flurry of jabs to the heart. Quinelle gasped and staggered away. The crowd yelled encouragements, shifting as the fight shifted, making room as Fargo shoved the big teamster back against a wagon wheel with a tattoo of brutal blows to the belly.

Quinelle shook off the effects of the punishing fists and by brute strength broke away from the wheel, bearing Fargo backward. He landed a left hook to Fargo's right eye, but again the smaller man dived in, coming up with his head against Quinelle's stomach and butting hard. Quinelle gagged and his mouth hinged agape. Fargo missed a wild knockout punch that would have ended the fight, his right fist grazing Quinelle's jaw, and he lurched past the man.

Again Quinelle was fast to react, taking full advantage of his opportunity by clobbering Fargo on the side of the head. Fargo reeled, seeing more stars than he usually did at night. Quinelle lunged in, grasping Fargo around the waist with his powerful arms, and lifted him up off the ground. Desperately Fargo twisted and writhed, wrestling to break loose, for this was the one hold that he had feared from the beginning of the fight. A killer bear hug.

The giant's arm tightened, driving the breath from Fargo's lungs. His arms were free, but with his feet off the ground he could not get any leverage to his punches. He struck Quinelle several times in the face, but the giant shoved his head against Fargo's chest and squeezed all the tighter. Fargo felt himself growing red in the face. The mob of teamsters and yardmen were cheering for Quinelle now.

He'd have to act quickly.

Fargo wedged both hands under Quinelle's chin and started to push. He lifted Quinelle's head up with his last remaining strength and began to shove it back, levering, bracing, knowing it was now a question of which man would break first. Feeling the power in the giant's arms, he suspected he would be the one to crack—at the spine, if not at the ribs—yet, in spite of feeling he was licked, he continued his grip on Quinelle's chin, thrusting the head far back.

Lights were dancing in his eyes now, and his heart was drumming. Then, suddenly, Quinelle released his grip and stumbled back, shaking his big head. Fargo's knees nearly gave in, but he managed to straighten himself. By the time Quinelle came at him again, he was breathing more easily. Three times he hit the giant in the body, the last time while Quinelle was hinging at the knees. Quinelle arched backward and his head struck the ground. He didn't get up.

"He dropped Tiny," a teamster muttered as others gaped and swore. The mulatto scratched his head as he saw the Canuck a few feet away on hands and knees, still panting for breath. "Damn if he didn't drop Henri, too!"

Fargo walked over to the smithy's rain barrel and splashed water on his face. He was surprised to discover that the knuckles of both hands were bleeding, and his ribs were still aching from the crush of Quinelle's encircling arms. He moved aside when Quinelle staggered up and plunged his head into the cool water. The big man looked up then, the water streaming from his face, and grinned.

"What horse you figure on ridin', mister?"

Fargo grinned, too. He stared out over the heads of the men clustering around them, glimpsing Jeppson, Delahay, and his daughter, whose face was stamped with cold disapproval.

"Okay, boys, now get to work," he called sharply, and the crowd began to break up.

When only Quinelle remained near the water barrel, drying his face with a burlap bag, Fargo asked him, "Why did you let go?"

Quinelle grimaced. "I reckon I didn't wish a busted neck."

Fargo smiled. At the time Quinelle had released him, he'd already begun to let up on the giant's head as his strength waned.

"The real reason," Fargo said.

Quinelle pushed back his wet hair with one huge hand, then said, "Well, I never seen a man come right out and pick a fight with me before. I figured you had balls."

"I guess we'll get along, Tiny." Fargo grinned again. "No hard feelings?"

"Nary a one. You snakin' our next outfit to the Crow?"

"M'name's Fargo, Skye Fargo. No misters." He dusted off his clothes and started toward the office. "Yeah, and I plan to bring the wagons through, too. The men who didn't want the last two to make it might like to stop us, so keep your eyes and ears open. If we can learn what we'll be up against, we can fight it."

"You got it. I'll pass the word. What about that horse?"

"You ride it," Fargo said, and continued on to the office building, halting under the windows while Delahay raised a sash.

"I believe you've handled teamsters afore, Mr. Fargo," Delahay said as he stuck his head out and chuckled admiringly.

"You are quite the brawler, all right," Bridget remarked acidly. "I suppose that's the best method of getting your men to work for you."

"No," Fargo replied, "it's only a custom of proving oneself—"

"There're other ways of proving oneself besides brawling." She shook her head angrily. "I saw you deliberately goad Tiny, just bully that poor man into fighting with you."

"Honey, you sound like you've never worked in a freight yard," Fargo retorted, keeping his temper in check. "One of the crew had to fight me, and Tiny was the biggest guy."

"At least I give you credit for that," she snapped, and ducked inside.

Delahay glanced over his shoulder at her and then looked out at Fargo again. "Bridget has her moods. You might tippytoe around her warpath for a while," he said apologetically. "And try to stay out of Chadwick's way for the short time before the outfit leaves."

Fargo laughed mirthlessly. "Luther Chadwick had better stop molesting my men," he responded, staring up at Delahay, "or I'll be looking him up myself."

2

Dusk was flaming beyond the black crags of the distant Laramie Mountains when Skye Fargo left Regina and returned to the heart of town. False-fronted honky-tonks, gambling halls, and dubious hotels lined shadowy Post Street, while on lanes and open tracts shanties and tents huddled in haphazard arrangements. A noisy confusion of trappers and rivermen, soldiers from the nearby fort, and immigrants en route to seek their fortunes all jostled one another along the dim boardwalks, money burning their pockets and thirst parching their throats.

Sweat-caked and begrimed after a day laboring in the wagon yard, Fargo headed for the barbershop to get his belated bath and trim. He winded through the evening throng, alert but not wary of those around him, listening to their passing laughter and spasmodic profanity with detached curiosity. So he paid no special attention when he first heard the quick steps behind him. Then, abruptly, he sensed a strange, almost menacing difference between them and everyone else's boot falls—a pattering approach that was very light and yet very intense, very similar to the pad of a stalking wildcat. It was now very close behind him.

Instinctively, Fargo pivoted aside. He was walking past the galleried, blank-walled storage shed adjoining a mercantile, but despite it being quite dark there, he caught a glimpse of shining steel and he heard a man grunt while stumbling forward, off balance.

In a dipping whirl, Fargo pawed for his revolver. He had hold of the butt and was beginning to unholster when the figure up ahead suddenly darted into a side alley. Running swiftly, Colt in hand, Fargo stared grimly down the alley. Too late. It was a pit of gloom into which the man had fled, and except for sound of racing footsteps retreating way down its length, there was no sign of him.

Fargo swore, released the hammer, and reholstered his weapon. It was then he discovered a rip in his buckskin jacket, where a razorsharp knife had slit the tough hide for an inch, an inch and a half, diagonally from the shoulder blade down around to the armpit seam.

The curses erupting then fairly blistered the air. After a last scathing glance into the murk where the knifer had vanished, Fargo moved on from the alley. He reached the end of the gallery and was crossing a vacant strip to the next block when two men came out of a saloon on the corner ahead and started toward him.

Spotting one another, they all paused, tensing.

One of the pair was knobby-thin and had the pointy face of a possum. His brown hair was long, his cheap range garb was dirty, and there was nothing prepossessing about him. Except that a sawed-off shotgun, of a style some fancied for brush work, was thonged with its double barrels downward under his thigh-length buffalo vest. Fargo would've recalled the man by his brush gun, if nothing else, but they hadn't met before. He knew the other man, though. Tully Nickles.

For a moment, it was a toss-up. Nickles had his hand hovering near his Colt Navy and was flexing his agile fingers. Fargo was bracing himself, watching Nickles like a cat eyeing a rat hole, while peripherally keeping tabs on the brush-gunner. The brush-gunner seemed to see something somewhere in back of Fargo. He nudged Nickles, and Nickles appeared to glimpse it too, abruptly relaxing his stance.

Fargo, suspecting trickery, waited until they began walking his way again before he craned to look behind him. Yonder was coming fat Marshal Oakes, moseying amiably on his rounds, preening one end of the graying mustache that drooped around his pudgy mouth and jowls. With a dry chuckle, Fargo turned and started ahead. Nickles was scowling, lips peeled and eyes slitted. The brush-gunner did not look mean or pleased or anything in between, just case-hardened indifferent.

"I'm not forgettin' your meddlin'," Nickles snarled.

"I wouldn't either, if I were you. Keep it in mind."

"Yeah, and you better keep your popgun handy."

"It's been handy a good many years," Fargo replied as he brushed by, adding as an afterthought: "And nobody can buy it."

He continued on to the barbershop, which was actually a large tent with a striped board propped out front. The rear was partitioned off for a tin plunge tub filled with tepid water guaranteed changed twice daily, whether it needed it or not. An hour after entering the tent, Fargo emerged clean and smelling of bay rum, leaving the barber complaining he'd have to change his bathwater a third time that day.

He then crossed the street, passed the noisy Rounders Saloon, and went into the Elite Café next door. The restaurant was a big, square room, the hubbub from the saloon echoing through their common wall and adding to the loud talk of patrons at its stubby tables.

The waitress came over, a cheery brunette around thirty. Her body was lush, perhaps a couple of years past its prime, but her legs were exquisite, and her full breasts and buttocks swelled her spangled green dress with sensual effect. Her eyes were sleepy and her nose was a bit long.

"Delores, I'm starved. Give me a hot, fast, lots-of meal."

"I'll go wave my apron in front of the open oven," she teased. "Next best dish is our dinner special, roast beef'n trimmings."

Fargo settled for the special. He ate hungrily, and after he'd finished, he stretched in his chair and remarked as she removed the plates, "I feel like a new man."

"I liked the feel of the old one. Do I see you later?"

"Maybe. Depends if there's time when I'm done working."

Delores didn't care for his answer. He wasn't wild about it either, but it was true. There were still plenty of details to attend to before the morning start, many that weren't his responsibility as wagon master, but that would become his problem en route if he didn't see to them now. The Conestogas were such relics, for example, that nobody else except Delahay knew the precise linchpin to use: a key factor in how much wear and strain were put on the wheel hubs and axles. And it was just fortunate that due to the traffic on the Oregon Trail, Fort Laramie had become the major stopover in the Rocky Mountain region to secure parts and repairs for any sort of wagon, at any time day or night.

Scrounging, Fargo located the linchpins and other needed stock. What with one thing and another, it took him past midnight to finish. By then the town was in full swing, gin mills and cribs booming, drunken rowdies and bluecoats reeling in the streets. Fargo, elbowing his way along, wedged through the raucous crush milling in front of the largest, the gaudiest of saloons, the Emperor Taproom & Social Club. As he was shoving by its main entrance, a bear of a man crashed out the batwings, arms windmilling, and sprawled on the boardwalk.

"Shit," Fargo muttered, frowning. "It's Tiny."

Quinelle scrambled to his feet, face flushed with drink. Two barrel-chested men with hard ruthless eyes stepped out and stood watchfully, shoulders hunched and hands fisted. The batwings behind them were being held open by rubberneckers, the most prominent of them being a middle-aged, middle-sized man in a brown town suit and string tie. There was Anglo-Saxon blood evident in his pale, angular face with its bony nose, pinched lips, and cold hazel eyes. Fargo sensed, just intuitively knew, that this was Luther Chadwick.

"Reckon I'll try that ag'in, gents," Quinelle declared blearily, wavering unsteady, "soon's you four stop dancin' about so fast."

His nose was bleeding and there were half a dozen more cuts on his face than Fargo recalled. A Starr Army .44, its grips turned forward for a right-hand draw, was under the waistband of his pants on the left side. He made no move toward his pistol, but staggered toward the doorway, fists balled, laughing good-naturedly. Brawling was his sport. Sober, Fargo suspected, he could have cracked the skulls of the two bar bouncers.

Quinelle fell into them. They split and went at him from either side, fists chopping at the drunken man's face. Still he laughed and swung his huge arms in wild arcs, one fist managing to catch the bouncer on the left, striking his jawline with a meaty thud. The bouncer arched backward and slid along the boardwalk planks, coming to rest when his head dropped off the edge into the gutter.

The other bouncer returned the favor by smacking Quinelle alongside the cheek with a round-house knuckler, momentarily stunning him. Before he could recover, the bouncer got an arm around him and smashed him twice in his injured nose with stiff, short-range punches. The fallen bouncer, meanwhile, groped about and picked up a broken whiffletree, one end iron-bound, from the muck. He lurched forward with this deadly weapon in his hand, blood pouring from his cut lips down onto his shirt front, murder flaring in his eyes.

"Not that," Fargo cautioned. "A fight's a fight."

The bouncer turned, mouth open. "I didn't ask you, pal."

"I'm telling *you*."

Quinelle and the second bouncer were wrestling in the doorway. Butting hard, Quinelle broke free and launched a one-two combination, his left opening a gash over the bouncer's eye, his right loosening a few teeth. Men were spewing out the windows and side door to watch the fight. Quinelle's hoarse laugh could be heard above their yells.

The bouncer with the whiffletree eyed the two. He glanced again at Skye Fargo. The men scuffling at the entrance staggered, entangling their feet, and Quinelle went down driving against the bouncer's knees and knocking him against the hitch rail. The bouncer with the club leapt forward, eyes glittering, aiming a kick at Quinelle's face while raising the whiffletree to brain him.

A revolver blasted. The bouncer screamed with pain and dropped the club, gripping his right forearm with his left hand. He stared at the blood seeping through his fingers, then at Fargo, who stood nearby, smoking Colt in hand. Hatred congealed in his eyes.

"Some folks sure won't listen," Fargo remarked languidly.

Quinelle was pummeling the other bouncer in the belly and face, punching him into submission. The bouncer sagged dazedly to his knees while the crowd closed in around them, baying for the finishing blow. They weren't disappointed. Quinelle brought his right fist up and hit the bouncer's chin with the sound heard in a slaughterhouse, when a steer was stunned with a maul. The bouncer was out before he landed. Quinelle stood catching his breath, looking at the wounded bouncer, then at where the bouncer was glowering. Then he spotted Fargo.

"C'mon Skye, I buy you a drink," Quinelle called, laughing.

"Skye?" Chadwick turned, peering at Fargo, then stepped out of the saloon. "You Skye Fargo, who whipped Tully Nickles?"

Fargo eased forward. "Yeah. You Luther Chadwick, who hired him?" he responded amiably. The crowd gave him room as he approached the curtly nodding man, then gathered around behind. Tiny Quinelle pushed up at Fargo's side, no longer smiling, but Fargo kept a hint of humor in his tones when he spoke. "From now on, Chadwick, I take a personal affront if anyone from Consolidated messes with Regina. Like Nickles tried to get away with doing this morning, understand?"

Chadwick shoved hands inside his coat pockets and rocked on the balls of his feet. "I dunno where you get off championin' Regina," he said harshly, "but I do know a stranger in town would play a much smarter game by keepin' his horn outta affairs that don't concern him."

"I'm the new wagon master at Regina." Fargo smiled, but there was a chill to his eyes. "I don't play games. I'm concerned about running the next outfit through, and about stopping whoever interferes with it or my crew—stopping them *dead* in their tracks. Remember that."

"Fargo, are you insinuatin' that I, that Consolidated . . . ?"

"Are crooked as a dog's hind leg? Why, perish the thought." Fargo shrugged. "I'm informing you, is all, for sake of our mutual interests." Parting with a wintry smile, he turned his back on Chadwick and pushed through the crowd.

Tiny Quinelle caught up within half a block. "Jeez, Skye, you really had Chadwick squirmin'. You shoulda called him out, then."

"Bull. He hoped I'd threaten or accuse him in public, without proof to back it. That'd get me jailed, with his clout, and that'd delay the next run, maybe for so long that Regina'd lose the contract." Fargo glanced at Quinelle. "And bulling me won't help your case."

"Aw, you got me wrong, boss. I was only followin' orders."

"When did I tell you to go on a drunken tear?"

"You tol' me to look an' listen, an' try learnin' what'll happen. I was. Naturally I couldn't snoop 'bout innercent without a drink."

"And naturally you chose a saloon by innocent chance."

"Not a'tall. The Consolidated muckers hang out at the Emperor, supposedly 'cause Chadwick owns a share of it. They slickered me into that rumpus. I didn't start it, honest. Somethin' else you oughta know," Quinelle said, lowering his voice to a whisper. "Don't look behind, but Grady's following us. I'll cut off at this upcomin' alley, loop 'round the back of the buildings, and pick him up ahead."

Fargo nodded grimly. It was problematical whether Chadwick had sent the stocky mule skinner, or whether Grady was acting on his own interests, to repay Fargo for having trounced him along with Nickles. He watched Quinelle duck into the alley and disappear at a sprint toward the rear of the building. In a moment he'd be coming up on Grady from behind. Crossing the next alley, Fargo glanced back out of the corner of his eye and caught a glimpse of Grady about thirty yards behind him, with another man in a plaid shirt hastening to catch up with him. No sign of Quinelle, however.

Casually yet discreetly, Fargo unholstered his Colt. Subtracting the shot he'd fired to nick the bouncer, the revolver was good for five more shots—and that would have to be good enough against the two armed men.

He strode along the next stretch of gallery until he felt that the men had also crossed the alleyway and were on the same boardwalk with him. He stopped suddenly then, heeled around, and started to walk toward them, reading the surprise in their faces. Grady stepped out into the street while the man in the plaid shirt hugged the wall of the shop alongside him. At the same instant, Fargo glimpsed Tiny Quinelle turning the corner of the alley behind them.

"You boys looking for me?" Fargo asked softly.

Grady's eyes shifted to the other man on the walk. One of them was bound to blast Fargo if they both opened fire together, catching Fargo in a cross trap before he could swing and plug them both—they might as well've painted their thoughts on signboards, Fargo observed, and hung them around their necks. He waited, poised, for them to make their play, while Quinelle settled himself at the alley.

Quinelle didn't wait, but called, "Hey, Grady."

Startled, Grady spun about. Quinelle was not over fifteen yards behind him, standing feet apart by the planked sidewalk, a small grin on his face. Grady read the pattern and dug for his pistol. At the same time the man in the plaid shirt dropped his right hand, Skye Fargo leapt to one side, then the twin bursts of Grady's and Quinelle's weapons exploded in flame and smoke, melding as one.

Fargo kept his eyes on his target. The man in the plaid shirt was lifting his pistol from the holster when Fargo triggered his Colt, and the man shuddered, dust puffing from his shirt where the slug drilled into his midriff. That didn't prevent him from completing his draw, though, his finger squeezing reflexively while he was dying on his feet. Fargo, dropping to the street, winced as a bullet slashed his left forearm.

Quinelle's big Starr thundered again. The man in the plaid shirt threw another hasty shot, but it went wide of the mark. Fargo leveled calmly and drove his man back against the wall, where he slumped, trying to straighten and shoot again. Fargo held his third shot as he watched the man fumbling to raise his pistol for the last time. The effort was useless. With a coughing gurgle, the man slid down to the walk, his head lolling to one side.

"That's all," Tiny Quinelle called from the corner, daubing his bullet-grazed earlobe. "Hey, looks like they got you."

"Nothing much," Fargo replied, shaking his head. He glanced at the man in the plaid shirt, then at Grady lying facedown in the dirt, and then at the crowd converging from the street and saloons. Among the gathering shouts and trampling boots, he spotted the red hair of Tully Nickles, who let out a bellow when he saw Fargo.

"Maybe not quite all," Fargo said to Quinelle. "But it'll be between me and Nickles. You can take anybody else who opens up."

Luther Chadwick suddenly dived out of the Emperor and grasped Nickles by the arm, halting him. An argument broke out, Nickles trying to shake loose and continue up the street, while Chadwick clung to him and refused to allow the showdown. Chadwick's reluctance was not due to fear, Fargo figured, and certainly not from any desire to see him stay alive. No, Chadwick must feel he had a better plan or a long-range scheme this could jeopardize.

Then Marshal Oakes came sprinting toward them, red-faced and a-wheeze like deflating bagpipes. Chadwick and Nickles retired to the Emperor, and Quinelle growled, "The party's over now for sure."

Hastening up, the marshal regarded both bodies and then eyed Fargo and Quinelle. "All right, is this some of Regina's handiwork?"

Fargo smiled thinly. "Self-defense. See their guns?"

"Self-defense," Oakes repeated as though begrudging the sound of it. "I'm of a mind to run you in anyhow, for disturbin' the peace and litterin' the street."

Quinelle stepped up close and loomed over him. "Try."

"I, er, I'll let you go this time. But you better watch your step 'round here," Oakes declared pugnaciously, "and in fact, you better clear out while you can. Chadwick mayn't be as understandin'."

"Any Consolidated boys who open up on us will get a dose of a lead, same as these two," Fargo said evenly. "And we're leaving when we're ready, Marshal."

"Your funeral," Oakes grumbled.

Fargo and Quinelle turned their backs and walked on up the street.

Quinelle grinned crookedly. "Where do we go next?"

"I want you to go to the wagon yard and sack out," Fargo ordered, then rubbed his chin thoughtfully. "Tell Tobac to add two more to his nighthawk crew. I want five men guarding the outfit, at least five, and they're to shoot anyone coming near."

"Okay, but what about you, that wound o' yours?"

"It's only a scratch, Tiny. I'll go get a bandage put on it and, well . . . I'll see you in the morning."

Quinelle lumbered away like a great St. Bernard dog.

Skye Fargo grinned after him, satisfied that Quinelle would be worth his weight in gold before the trip was over. Fargo had met his kind on the trail before—reckless, shiftless, heavy-drinking *hombres* who'd give their lives for the men earning their respect and trust.

3

The Elite Café was closed, but the Rounders resounded with alcohol-fed noise. Fargo strode by, keeping a wary lookout, and cut into the entrance of the hotel above the saloon. He climbed the steep, rickety staircase that led to the upper landing, went along the dimly lit corridor, and stopped in front of Room 14.

"Delores?" He rapped on the door. "Open up."

There was a padding of feet, then her voice. "Who's that?"

"Skye."

"I don't know no Skye. I used to once know a Skye, but stopped thinkin' of him hours ago and went to bed. Now, go away, y'hear?"

"Let me in, Delores. I'm hurt."

Silence. Utter, implacable silence.

"For god's sake, Delores, I'm out here wounded and—"

"We've all our share of broken hearts, bucko, so suffer."

"Not that kind! I've got a flesh wound. Open the door."

"I most certainly will not."

"I'll kick it in."

The inside bold shot back. Delores opened the door like a gust of wind and stared at Fargo half in dismay, half in defiance. "This better not be a trick to get in my good graces—and britches."

"Look at the floor," he replied, entering. "You see blood?"

Delores slammed the door. "Blood. So?" She planted two fists on her hips, her breasts swelling beneath her floor-length, pale-violet Mother Hubbard nightgown. "I waited and waited instead of going out, and if you think you can waltz in at—"

"My blood, dammit! You got anything to bind me up?"

"Oh, no, I don't cater to them perversions. If you like roping—"

"My arm, Delores, my arm's bleeding and needs a bandage."

Delores gazed at his left arm, eyes widening as she spotted the blood seeping down over his hand and trickling off his fingertips. "Well, why didn't you say so? C'mere, dearie, take off your shirt and things and sit down here on my bed. I'll fix it."

Fargo removed his hat and jacket while Delores began rummaging in the bottom drawer of her bureau. Then, loosening his pants so he wouldn't have to fight the long shirttails, he gingerly peeled off his blood-encrusted shirt and studied his wound. It was a clean furrow along the fleshy part of his forearm, causing considerable bleeding, but no real injury. He sat down on the edge of her bed and watched her pour water into a basin and carry it over, along with a jar of iodoform powder and a few clean rags.

"Was it a husband or merely a fiancé who shot you?" Delores asked as she bathed the wound.

Fargo told her what happened and why, recapping his day and adding the news that he'd be leaving in the morning.

When she'd poured the iodoform on the wound and wrapped it, she surveyed her handiwork and said with a sense of satisfaction, "There, that'll hold you. I wish I could, for more'n tonight."

Fargo leaned back and grinned at her. She was perched on the bed, so close that he could feel her warm breath against his skin and smell the fragrance of her perfume. She was trembling; she stroked a finger shakily across his bare chest and stomach and murmured, "I've got a flesh wound, too. I'm hurtin' all over."

"I'll fix it," Fargo murmured, chuckling, and untied the ribbon at the neck of her gown.

Delores rose, her pink tongue gliding across her lips. Slowly, tauntingly, she shrugged the gown off and let it blossom down around her feet. Then she crawled naked on the bed, her body firm and slim-waisted, her breasts globular and hard-nippled. She cupped her breasts invitingly. "You can greet them if you like. They're family."

"Kissing cousins?" Fargo said, his mouth closing on one of the nipples, sucking while he fondled her other breast. His other hand roamed down her body to the vee of her crotch. She brought her thighs together on his hand and held it there, squeezing.

"We're forgetting something," she said huskily.

Pulling away, Fargo hastened to be rid of his clothes. Delores watched him tug off his boots and pants, her eyes growing smoky and hungry as she gazed at his manhood. They stretched, then, close alongside each other. Fargo gliding his hand down over the smoothness of her buttocks while Delores spread her legs slightly to allow him to caress her sensitive valley. She moved her hips a little in concert with his rubbing hand, and soon she was so moist that he was able to ease three fingers up inside her.

She moaned, her hand sliding between his legs in search of his swelling erection. "It's my turn tonight," she sighed, stroking his shaft. "And my turn is coming up."

Then she climbed on top of Fargo, undulating as she gently lowered herself, slowly enveloping his turgid length until she squatted, her pubic bone pressing against his. And then she jumped, impaling herself on him forcefully as she came down. Delores hovered above him, thrusting with her hip and buttock muscles, pumping on his hardened girth as fast as she could, pummeling Fargo against the bed.

His hands grasped her dancing breasts. "Not so hard!"

"Oh, your poor arm," she cooed, slowing.. "I'm sorry. You just lie there and let me take you nice and easy."

Despite her intentions, Delores soon began humping wildly again, bouncing her hips up and down with increasing abandon. She pistoned her tightly gripping loins around his shaft until the bedsprings squealed in protest, until Fargo was no longer aware of his wound and was thrusting in rhythm to her frenzied tempo.

He sucked one swaying breast into his mouth, flicking her distended nipple with his tongue and grasping her other breast with his hand. Her passion continued building to an insane pitch. She writhed and wriggled and squirmed in a dozen different directions. Fargo felt his excitement mounting higher and sensed he was on the brink of release. Her lustrous hair was a dizzying cloud in his eyes, the tang of her sweat was on his tongue, her dilated gaze glowed with ecstasy as, together, they hammered at yet a faster pace, pushing deeper, their sweating bodies slapping and rubbing tempestuously.

Delores tried to say something, but she could no longer speak. She moaned, shivering from the electric impact of her own orgasm, as the hot jets of Fargo's bursting climax flooded up into her belly. He pulled her tighter to his pulsing groin, as if he were trying to merge flesh and bone.

Then he collapsed, exhausted and drained. She fell across him, stretching her legs back so she could lie with him inside her. They dozed off, their bodies gently intertwined.

Fargo awoke once, briefly, to a bunch of drunken revelers serenading outside the saloon. When he shifted, Delores rolled off him and curled against his side, murmuring in her sleep. It was still dark, but he didn't know the time and really didn't care. As soon as the carolers staggered on, he fell back asleep.

He awoke a second time to a slight scraping noise against the side of the building. He rose, slipping from the bed and easing toward the window, his bare feet noiseless on the floor. Delores felt his absence anyway and opened her eyes. When she sat up, still foggy with sleep, Fargo put a finger to his lips as a signal for silence and pointed to the window with his other hand.

Delores froze, breathless. For an agonizing moment they heard nothing, and Fargo guessed it was probably sometime around four in the morning, in that predawn stillness when everybody is sleeping their soundest, and those awake are at their most relaxed. The best time to mount a sneak attack.

Then, from below the window, came a soft squeak of stressed wood. Fargo was beside the window now, poised motionless, staring intently at the drawn blind. The sash creaked, slowly rising, and the blind began to quiver.

A hand raised the bottom edge of the blind. Whoever was out there then stuck his other hand underneath, gripping two sticks of black powder tied together, fuses sparking and hissing.

Fargo pounced. He grabbed hold of those two hands by their wrists and thrust them out the window, leaning way out before letting go with a final shove. The black powder sticks went with them, and so did the blind, ripping off its roller to flap out like a flying tail.

A startled howl, which had begun at the height of the window, was swiftly falling away and down. Fargo, peering out the window, saw a tall, spindly ladder teetering in an arc away from the building wall, its legs firmly rooted in the alley below. The hunching silhouette of a man was perched on its top rungs, clinging helplessly as he was catapulted backward toward the structure on the opposite side of the alley, which just so happened to be the town marshal's stone office and cellblock.

The ladder struck the edge of the structure, toward the rear where the jail cells would be. The man, whom Fargo had never seen before, was flung onto the roof, his howl cut off as the sticks detonated with a terrific, brilliant flash. The hotel quivered, glass shattered, while down across the alley, the rear quarter of the marshal's office hurtled out, stone, beams, and masonry cycloning up and about in a blinding white cloud. The roof collapsed in the hole the explosion had punched, fire blossoming through the wreckage.

By the suddenly sprouting incandescence, Fargo saw Marshal Oakes stumble out the front door, wearing long red underwear and nothing else. Other doors and windows were opening, the street swirling in a confusion of shouting men and women both dashing about, cursing and questioning, gaping at the ruined building that was now being consumed by hungry flames.

Fargo turned, surveying Delores. "Are you all right?"

She nodded, though she was shaking a little, still dazzled by the glare and blast. "Somebody doesn't like me," she said, smiling weakly. "I can't imagine who."

"No, it was me he was after. I must've been followed or traced here, not a hard thing to do, but I should've thought ... I never should've risked ..." He paused, angrily slamming the window. "If I hadn't been lucky enough to hear that ladder brushing up against the wall, he would've succeeded," Fargo said grimly as he started back to Delores. "But I think that's all he'll try for tonight."

"You mean for forever," Delores remarked. "Now, stop the ifs, the blaming yourself, and come to bed."

Fargo did, cradling Delores tenderly to him. He listened to the continuing noise from the street and watched the reflection of the fire in the wavy glass pane of her window, and he wondered what tomorrow day would bring in the way of death.

Fargo lay there quite a spell before going to sleep again.

4

Fargo stopped in the next morning at the office of Regina. Just before he went inside, Bridget Delahay greeted him with a curt nod.

"I heard about last night," she said slowly. "Please be more careful, Mr. Fargo."

"Because this load must go through?" He grinned. "Nothing else?"

"That's enough," she murmured, but he saw her face redden slightly. "Incidentally," she continued, "you're taking a passenger through to the Crow River post."

"Who?"

"Me."

Fargo laughed. "Not this load," he stated flatly. "It'll be no place for a woman."

"I've gone with outfits before," she retorted stiffly.

"Not when I was wagon master. Forget about it." Fargo entered the office, and when he shook hands with Justin Delahay, he told the older man,

"Your daughter wants to ride along with the train."

Delahay nodded gloomily. "I don't like to do it, either."

Fargo stared. "You mean she's to go?"

"I can't go myself, and somebody has to sign papers to renew the contracts. I hope I can depend on you for her safety."

"No one's safe on this run, no one! We'll be looking for trouble all along the line. The crowd that broke up your first two outfits will be laying for this one, knowing they'll have to stop it," Fargo protested, hearing Bridget come in behind him and stand by the door. "There's no other way? Couldn't I sign for the company?"

"The army wouldn't accept your signature. Colonel Garabedian can't deal with anyone 'cept an actual agent or part owner of the company, and Bridget is an officer." Delahay smiled at his daughter while he spoke. "Bridget has handled transactions before. I can depend upon her to see to Regina's best interests."

"I promise to stay out of your way, Mr. Fargo," Bridget said acridly. "Like it or not, however, I shall be going."

"As you will." Fargo clamped his hat down on his head and strode out of the office, slamming the door behind him.

He went into the wagon yard, over to where he'd tied his Ovaro pinto, and stood checking his gear, tightening the latigo harshly, while he scanned the yard and let his exasperation fade. The crew was hitching up the wagons. By the time the breed named Carajou backed the final pair of wheelers into their traces, Fargo had calmed considerably.

"Let's go, you skinners. Carajou, you drive the first wagon. Brea, on the tail. Velázquez, you're good with horses, you wrangle the cavvy. Rest of you, fall in as you fit in, and keep to that order."

Shortly the Regina train was heading through Fort Laramie. To volleys of popping whips, oaths, and "Gee up, thar! Gee up!" seventeen aging freighters rumbled through the dust, wheels sinking deep into the street bed, five teams of mules to each wagon. The seventeen mule skinners rode on wagon-box seats, and from their perches they made as much of a show as they could, bellowing and snapping the drive reins and cracking their blacksnakes. On the last wagon with Brea sat Upwind Muldoon, the outfit's cook, whose nickname Fargo had learned was due to his soda biscuits having the same effect as beans. Bridget Delahay rode the lead wagon—as Fargo figured she'd pick, though, *of course*, that had nothing to do with his choice for lead driver, Carajou, whose grubby duds made believable his boast that he didn't change clothes till they rotted off him. Fargo, asaddle the Ovaro with the white midsection and black fore- and hindquarters, trotted along the line of wagons and wondered if he could get four hours' march out of the mules before needing rest and water. The teams already looked as if they'd collapse if their traces didn't hold them up.

The train rolled by the Emperor Taproom & Social Club, where a large crowd had gathered to watch. Fargo saw Luther Chadwick smoking a fat torpedo cigar, hands thrust into his vest pockets.

The Consolidated owner stared at him, and Fargo could read the ruthlessness in his cold black eyes; Chadwick was the type of man who had to have his own way or die.

Next to Chadwick stood Tully Nickles, his nose encased in strips of white adhesive. Beside the redhead was the scrawny brush-gunner, who watched Fargo steadily, as if measuring him. Nickles was anything but impassive, throwing back his head and laughing nastily.

"Look at them cussed fools! Two outfits wiped out, now drivin' smackety-dab into cholera, with the Crow and Sioux on the warpath, an' they thinks Fargo'll get through with them clapped-out Connies!"

"Eh, *toi con*," Henri the Canuck shouted violently. "We could take these wagons to the moon and back with barefoot teams."

Fargo spurred his pinto up beside Henri's freighter. "Shut up, Henri, and keep on going. We give them the pleasure of a fight, we may end up stopped here before we've started. And that's no way to handle a whip," he charged, standing in his stirrups, leaning and snatching the blacksnake away from a very startled Henri. "Sloppy as hell, Henri. This is how you should let her rip."

The lash streaked behind him as Fargo reared to make his foreward cast. He was at the proper distance for the tip to snap just under Tully Nickles' nose. With a howl, the redhead clapped both hands to his cut mouth, the quick blood showing through his fingers, while he averted his face and whirled around.

"Sorry," Fargo yelled contritely, turning in his

saddle. "Hey, if you'd said something, I'd have known you were there in back of me."

The whip was cracking forward now, swinging with Fargo as he turned, and lapping out like a furious tongue. It caught Nickles a hard, slashing blow across the tight seat of his trousers.

"I'm afire," Nickles howled. "I'm afire!"

Tully Nickles was actually on fire. Fargo saw smoke pluming from the right hip pocket of the man's trousers as he plunged through the crowd—living proof that a gent could get himself into trouble by always carrying a block of Chinese matches in a hip pocket. The whip had struck just right, igniting one or two of the matches in the block, and the rest had instantly burst into flame. Squalling louder with pain and slapping furiously at his seat at every springing jump he took, Nickles dived headlong into the nearest horse trough.

Post Street resounded with guffawing laughter, drowning out Fargo's apology for his second accident with the whip. Shrugging, Fargo handed it back to Henri, who almost dropped it, he was hooting so hard.

Fargo moved up to the next wagon, driven by Quinelle. "You see the small guy with the brush gun, Tiny? Do you know who he is?"

Quinelle glanced back and nodded. "Sorta. His name's Reed, Devin Reed. We run across him out on the trail a coupla days afore Abe McHugh got lead poison."

"I thought McHugh was scalped," Fargo said. "A Sioux raid."

Quinelle chuckled bitterly. "They wasn't Injuns," he snapped. "One of 'em had a mustache.

They run off our stock, an' when Abe went after 'em, he got into an ambush. He had ten bullets in him an' his top was gone."

"They get the wagons, too?"

"Oh, sure. When we was chasin' the stock, another party of 'em came in behind and burned up all the equipment and cargo."

Fargo looked back at the brush-gunner named Devin Reed. Undoubtedly, Chadwick had used Reed the last time in attacking and gutting McHugh's outfit. Reed said something to Chadwick and then the Consolidated owner tossed away his cigar and went to help Nickles.

"Reed's fast with that scattergun, too," Quinelle added. "If we meet up with him ag'in on the trek, Capt'n, we'd best shoot first."

"I intend to," Fargo said.

The skinners broke into the old "Root Hog or Die" song as they rolled out of town. Fargo listened thoughtfully, surveying the plodding line, then caught up with the head of the train. He tipped his hat politely, Bridget nodded, and Carajou motioned to him to come closer to the lead wagon so he could ask a question.

"Say, Capt'n, how far d'you figure we'll get tonight?"

Fargo shrugged. "We can make fifteen miles. Maybe twenty, depending on the mood of these flea-bitten mules, and that'll take us down to Eureka Springs with time to spare."

"I like your notionin'," Carajou replied, mulling. "To go by way o' the Springs means we're cutting due south, jus' goin' right on through instead o' follerin' the zigs'n zags o' Chugwater Creek." He paused and spat into the dust of the road. "It'll put us outta the Goshen Hole area in two days 'stead o' four, an' that's to the good, though it do leave us at mercy of the long grass after that."

"Long grass?"

"It burns, Capt'n, burns like almighty hell."

Fargo nodded. "Thanks, Carajou, I'll bear it in mind."

"I ain't aimin' to fry myself," Carajou told him pointedly.

Outside Fort Laramie, near the junction of the Laramie and North Platte rivers, they struck out overland. A hardscrabble landscape spread endlessly before them, a rumpled tawny-brown blanket thatched with short grasses, brush thickets, and scrub trees, and splattered with violet, purple and burnt orange. A curving, saw-toothed line along the western horizon outlined the Laramie Mountains, while eastward and ahead, a trackless plain diminished to a faint crease and finally disappeared altogether.

The train soon fell into the fairly standard routine of halting at midmorning, noon, and midafternoon, watering and then feeding the mules in long canvas troughs to prevent any waste of grain. During these rest breaks, Fargo left the train to scout the immediate area, riding a cautious circuit and then climbing the highest rise and stopping to watch and listen. Toward sunset, they entered a patch of scarps and gullies, which soon broadened into a small pocket valley shaded by lofty cottonwoods and box elders. At one end was a wide, shallow pool, and in an adjacent field of bluestem grass, they pitched camp for the night. As far as they could tell, they had Eureka Springs to themselves—but Fargo didn't plan to take that for granted.

Dinner talk was desultory, the men fatigued. Tobac stood with his nighthawk crew around the campfire, drinking coffee from big tin cups before going out on duty.

Fargo walked over to them and said, "We'll be keeping most of the stock inside the circle at night, but we won't be able to accommodate the extra animals. Graze them close."

The nighthawks agreed, although they showed some surprise. It was the custom to let all stock out to graze at the end of a day's haul and drive them into the wagon enclosure early the next morning for hitch-up.

"When does the team stock get to graze?" Tobac asked.

"We'll start an hour later each morning," Fargo explained. "We can run them outside the corral and keep a close watch on them in the daylight. If Chadwick strikes at us, it's liable to be through the animals first. Without them, we'd be stalled flat."

Leaving the nighthawks, Fargo made his round of the corral. The wagons were drawn up in the shape of a huge horseshoe, the front wheels of each Conestoga chained to the rear wheels of the one in front of it, tongues turned inward. The most ferocious Texas longhorn would have a difficult time breaking out of the enclosure.

Moving through the darkness, Fargo heard Bridget Delahay's voice calling him from her wagon. When he went over, she asked, "Must we suffer the livestock inside the compound tonight?"

"Tonight," Fargo answered, "and every night."

"I cannot believe we're in such danger as to warrant it," she retorted. "The Sioux wouldn't dare attack this close to Fort Laramie. Perhaps after we pass Council Crest, but not yet."

"Perhaps not even then. The Sioux have been kicking up more of a fuss recently, but if they come onto us, chances are it'll be to beg or trade, or steal. But it's not the red devils I'm worried about," Fargo said, terse-lipped. "It's the white ones."

Bridget eyed him steadily. "I stand corrected. You seem to know your business, I'll grant you, but then, that's why Dad hired you. Regina needs someone who knows how to play Luther Chadwick's kind of fight. Someone who's as hard and merciless as Chadwick himself."

Fargo listened to that and felt the young woman's words bite into him. He cursed inwardly, angered by the judgment she and her father had placed on him. Yet, strangely, at the same time he felt a liking for the Delahays, an admiration for the courage and spirit they displayed, and a respect for them that he didn't feel toward many.

He touched his hat brim. "Thanks a heap, ma'am."

Her eyes sparked. "Don't call me ma'am," she snapped. "I'm younger than you, unmarried, and figure on remaining so."

"Now that I think we all can believe." Fargo winked, and started on. "Excuse me, I want to go check if anyone else is riding my ass."

He saddled a fresh horse from the cavvy, preferring to let his Ovaro remain at graze after its all-day jaunt, and rode out of camp. Leaving

Eureka Springs on the other side of the pocket valley, Fargo made a wide circuit, picked up the trail the outfit had made, and followed it back toward Fort Laramie. For several hours he rode at a fast trot along the tracks.

It was nearly midnight when he spotted a small spot of light on the horizon a mile or two northeast of the wagon trail, and veering toward it, he watched closely, seeing the light flicker and surmising it was a campfire and not some bright star.

Cautiously, covertly he approached, dismounting when he was within a few hundred yards of the little fire. There were no trees on the open plain and he had to hobble his horse and creep forward on foot. He heard another horse whinny, then his own mount whinny in response, and he froze to the ground, hand on the butt of his revolver, listening, wishing he had ridden his trained Ovaro instead.

There were no other sounds.

Crawling closer, Fargo could make out a dozen or more horses hobbled on the plains. Again he paused, waiting for fully ten minutes, hoping that a cigarette light or a movement of some kind would reveal a guard. Evidently no one had been assigned night duty from the camp, which struck Fargo as unusual but not impossible.

He slowly eased on, the flames almost down to embers by the time he closed to twenty feet of the fire. Now he could make out saddle gear and other camp supplies lying scattered about, and the silhouettes of sleepers rolled in sugans, feet toward the hot coals.

A man sat up in his blanket, kicked it away, and

climbed to his feet. Fargo heard him curse softly as he stumbled over something, then the sound of the man relieving himself. He returned, tossed a few buffalo chips on the coals, and stood for a moment poking the fire. By the flare of renewed flames, Fargo saw that the man was Devin Reed, the brush-gunner. The men on the ground, though, remained indistinguishable.

Fargo, however, had seen enough by seeing Reed, and didn't need more to confirm his suspicions. Reed was settling in his sugan when Fargo began crawling back through the stubby grass. He moved again past the hobbled horses and was almost to his mount when he heard it snort and paw dirt. He stopped abruptly. His horse, a deep-brisketed bay, was standing a dozen yards away—standing very stiffly.

Carefully Fargo lowered himself in the scrubby growth, reaching at the same time for his revolver, unholstering it without a sound. Then he waited, pressed facedown, breathing easily. There was little doubt in his mind now that Devin Reed's band had posted a guard and that he'd heard the horse whinny a while before. He'd come around to investigate, and he was lying in the ground cover just ahead—possibly not more than a few feet away.

Fargo grinned coldly, caressing with his fingers the smooth butt of his Colt. This was a game of patience, and he realized the man who made the first move might likely make his last.

He played the game for over half an hour, fighting down once a terrible temptation to sneeze. Eventually his patience was rewarded, the figure of a man starting to rise gradually, first his low-crowned hat showing above the grass. He was about eight feet away.

Fargo hunkered flat, drawing his knees in under him and digging the toes of his boots into the earth. His left hand settled on the cool surface of a stone embedded in the earth, and after a little surreptitious prying, he managed to work it loose. Then, still keeping low, he wrist-flicked the rock in a skittering toss to his left. The instant it landed, the man swiveled, a pistol blasted, and a bullet ripped through the grass where the stone had fallen.

In a crouching sprint, Fargo tore across the intervening space. He slashed twice with the barrel of his revolver and heard the man scream in pain as he went down, though it was too dark to see where the heavy steel had chopped against flesh. In two more leaps he caught up with his hobbled bay, slipped the knot, and sprang into the saddle, spurring his horse into a vaulting gallop.

The camp was in immediate uproar, and the gun-whipped man in the grass was writhing and swearing, lisping as if some front teeth had been knocked out or removed. Fargo neck-reined his bay in a pinwheeling turn, jabbing it harder in the ribs, and surged straight through the camp, yelling loudly and firing his revolver. He heard the men scramble frantically behind him, confused and routed and, Fargo hoped, without their weapons. He then tore southward in a direct heading for the Regina wagon train. Behind him, a few of the jostled sleepers were beginning to fire pistols and rifles, but in the chaos their bullets either went astray or hit their own still-hobbled and unsaddled horses. Fargo kept on racing away.

It was nearly dawn when Fargo reached the corral. Most of the crew was either getting up or out chousing the stock, while Upwind Muldoon was fixing to give the call for breakfast. They acknowledged Fargo but didn't ask any questions, although Tiny Quinelle remarked, "Reckon you might climb inna my wagon, boss, and catch some shut-eye."

Fargo took the suggestion to heart. He waited till the outfit was rolling and sunrise was streaking the eastern skyline, by which time he'd traded the hard-ridden bay for his Ovaro. He had some of the cook's flapjacks, which were beginning to earn the same notoriety as his biscuits. Then, tying his horse behind Quinelle's freighter, Fargo ducked through the rear canvas flap and found a spot to stretch out amid the dense, dark welter of crates, casks, and other cargo.

He'd barely closed his eyes when Bridget Delahay trotted up on a chestnut mare she'd brought along. "Hello, in there," she called.

Fargo lifted his head slightly and looked out the tailgate. "Good morning, Miss Delahay. On a fresh-air constitutional, are you?"

Ignoring his comment, she scolded, "You should do your sleeping at night."

"Next time I'll be sure to ask you when I should sleep." Grinning, Fargo lay back down and slid his hat over his face, hearing Bridget gallop away.

It was high noon when he awoke. On his Ovaro again, he rode up alongside the wagon to thank Quinelle.

Quinelle asked, "Find anything last night?"

"As much as I expected," Fargo answered enigmatically.

They continued on long into dusk before making a dry camp for the night, watching the sunset enshroud the flatland. Then, watching the sunrise retorch the same endless expanse, they once again began their creeping journey down through the section commonly known as Goshen Hole. After their midday rest, however, the terrain gradually changed, softening, fertile though sunparched meadows more frequent now. By evening of this, the third day, fields of wheel-high grass stretched from the Laramie Mountains foothills on the west to the Nebraska boundary and beyond on the east.

They halted that night on the north side of Bear Creek, a shallow, weedy snake of water about thirty yards across. Fargo scanned the dry brown terrain along the creek, choosing his campsite carefully, finally selecting a gradual slope thirty yards up from the streambed.

When the wagons were rolled into their horseshoe circle and the teams unhitched, Carajou slipped his chains from the freighter and prepared to fasten his wheels.

"No," Fargo called sharply, "no chains tonight."

Carajou blinked. "We're not to deadlock the wagons?"

"Brakes only. Pass the word on down the line, will you?"

Bridget overheard him while climbing from the freighter. "Not chaining is worse than carelessness, Mr. Fargo. It's negligent."

"It's my order, not your concern." He watched Bridget stalk vexedly toward the creek, then signaled Velázquez and Tobac to come over, telling them, "All the stock and cavvy are to be kept close-herded by water's edge. You'll know what to do if anything happens."

Velázquez nodded. "*Entiendo*. The grass worries you, no?"

"Like Carajou said, I don't aim to get fried."

Fargo also had a strip of grass cut and piled near the campfire, and set extra guards for the night. He was seated on his bedroll, eating a late dinner, when Bridget approached, frowning at the grass.

"Haystacks instead of chains. I think you're foolish."

Setting his plate down, Fargo opened his war bag, removed a pair of clean denims, and held them up to her. "Here, try these on for size."

"Now you're absurd. They're far too big to fit me."

"Remember that. Then maybe you won't forget so easily that I wear the pants of this outfit, and you promised to stay out of them."

"Oh, I would if I could," she replied haughtily. "But I can't when a person of your rascally habits leads our men into silly, risky, and lax behavior."

"Rasc— You don't know my habits, honey. You don't even know me."

"I know *of* you. I've eyes; I saw you. I've ears, and I've heard more than I need or wish to about your incessant drunken brawls."

"Christ. Do you hear any fighting or see any liquor along?"

"Not yet. I've found no female stowaways either, other than a Delores Voght," Bridget replied tartly. "She tried to sneak aboard before we left town, while you were claiming your horse at the livery, and her confidences to me were shocking. I warn you, I'll resist any such lewd advances by you even if I must lock on a chastity belt."

"Suit yourself." Fargo picked up his plate. "But protecting a penny bank in a safe vault doesn't make it worth stealing, you know."

"Ohh! If you were a gentleman—"

"I am, with a lady. Listen, I don't care what you think, I said I'd do my damnedest to bring this train through, and I plan to."

"I hope you're able to keep your word." Tilting her nose and hiking her dress hem, Bridget again stomped off.

Fargo shook his head. "Sweet Jesus . . ."

Three hours before dawn, Tobac rousted him from his bedroll. "Boss, you said if anythin' happens I'd know what to do. I don't."

"What's wrong?"

"Call me barmy if it ain't growin' hot and cloudin' over."

Fargo sprang up. "You're okay. The wind must've shifted.

The moment of reckoning, Fargo thought.

It was bound to happen. Fargo had been expecting it, though he would've liked some forewarning of exactly when. But that would've required a constant watch of Devin Reed's bunch following the train, and Fargo hadn't any teamsters he felt could scout and be fully trusted. Sure, up till now they'd stuck by Regina. Quinelle was their acknowledged segundo, the strongest among them, and he'd declared his support. And, yeah, they had their scores to settle with Consolidated. Yet maybe one or so of them were staying under orders to spy for Chadwick; others before them had taken Chadwick's fat bribes. Even if none had sold out, they were sullen, each-for-himself rumdums, skittish as snake-boogered nags by fear of cholera and of Indians. Under pressure, they might well spook back into their old nature—if at first you don't succeed, haul your ass out before it gets shot off.

Anticipating this had stalked Fargo since Fort Laramie, cautioning what and how he spoke and acted. Now it was upon them. The moment of reckoning was here.

5

Fargo could feel the unusual heat of a breeze soughing in from the north. Out that way he could see a cloudy haze, at first an indistinct smear no bigger than a low prairie hillock, which swelled quickly, seemingly within seconds, to a heavy black smudge against the softer dark of the night sky. The expanding plume blotted the northern stars, yet as it billowed nearer, hotter, Fargo glimpsed new stars sparking to life in the pall, forming a groundline of flickering glows about two hundred yards distant—and closing fast.

He sniffed deeply, then swore under his breath. "They were waiting all night till the wind blew toward us, damn them. That grass is burning like tinder. Help me get everybody up, Tobac, *pronto!*"

Scooping large armfuls of grass from the piles, they rushed to the smoldering campfire and threw the grass on the banked coals. Immediately it ignited, flaring brilliantly in a swift rage of flame, illuminating the enclosure. Bleary-eyed men rolled stumbling from beneath the wagons, blinking querulously at the campfire, then turning with awakening alarm to stare at the advancing black cloud. It was shot through with ugly red streaks that consumed the scrubby brush and sere brown grasses in its path, the smoky blaze like a looming crimson hunger inexorably sweeping in to devour the wagon train.

"Drive the stock into the creek," Fargo shouted.

Tobac, his nighthawks, and a handful of teamsters raced to comply. The mules were plunging and kicking, white-eyed and ears laid back, and it took all the men's wits and strength to gather the fractious mules and head them toward water. From up the creek they heard a few gunshots and faint cussing yells, indicating Velázquez and his wranglers were attempting the same drive with the cavvy. And everywhere fear was in the air, fear and stampede.

"Turn your wagons around," Fargo ordered. "Into the water! Move 'em! Move 'em!" Another half-dozen men grasped the wheels of a wagon and turned it about so the Conestoga faced the creek. Fargo caught a peripheral glimpse of Bridget running toward him. But he had no time for her now, his attention focusing on the freighter.

"Get a man on the seat," he called out. "Brake it as it rolls!"

The skinners quickly realized what he meant. All the wagons were parked on the gentle incline at the crest of the shallow bank, and it required but a little push to start them rolling down toward the creek of their own volition. And this the crew began doing, hastily so, for the roaring ring of fire was now only seventy-five yards away, smoke and soot and crackling flames leaping into the sky as far as the eye could see. The heat was intense. Burning embers rained around the men as they worked to turn one wagon after another around and send rumbling down the grade into the water.

Skye Fargo sped from spot to spot, shouldering here, pushing there, trying to rally the men and stifle their panic. And before each wagon was shoved on its way, he made sure plenty of weapons and spare ammo were unloaded and passed around.

"The fire was torched, and somebody might use it as a screen to attack us," he explained. "They'll figure we're routed, unarmed, easy pickings. Well, they'll be the ones in for a surprise, if we keep cool heads and guns handy."

He continued shouting orders and encouragements until he could no longer be heard for the roar of flames. Wind drove pungent smoke down over them, then it lifted again and swept it high. It was then that a number of the men perceived the outlines of riders behind the flames, though they were unable to discern whether they were white men or Indians.

"They're gonna be fuckin' dead men," Brea declared.

"We better be ready for 'em," Henri the Canuck said, "when this fire gets down to the water. They'll try to hit us then."

More than half the wagons were already rolling into the water, their dirty white covers almost invisible in the smoke. Wooden wagons on wooden wheels, so age-dried and weathered that they were scarcely fit for more than kindling. The fire was encroaching at a furious pace, striking high into the air, the remaining patch of unburned ground seeming pitifully small, getting smaller, too small.

More than once the men glanced in terror, redoubling their efforts to salvage the rest of the wagons, stomping at new little fires with their boots.

"The crick ain't big 'nuff. The water'll boil off."

"It's big enough, deep enough. It only looks little."

"The fire'll jump, it's gonna jump, I tell you."

"Shit on a shingle, why don't the wind die down?"

Horses and mules neighed in fright, then began to dance and scream as the crackle of flames grew nearer. The flames seemed to lick at their very heels. The wall of fire and smoke obscured the world, adding to the oppressive horror. The sixteenth wagon rolled clear when the inferno was a mere thirty yards away. Four men, Fargo included, raced after the last freighter. They espied Bridget just ahead of them, angling for the water, suddenly stumbling as she ran.

As if Bridget's fall were a signal, the riders behind the fire abruptly began shooting through the flames. The teamsters scrambled to grab up their weapons, dive behind what little cover there was along the bank, and respond with lead salvos of their own. Most all were triggering carbines, but rarely had Fargo seen such an amazing variety of long iron in one compact group. There were Spencers .56-50s, of course, and Henry .44s; yet Fargo had also spotted a Burnside, a Gallagher, Maynard, Cosmopolitan, Ballard, and a damn-fool infantry Long Tom .47-70 with a 40-inch barrel. He felt in good company when he gave Quinelle his Sharps "big fifty" buffalo rifle to hold, while he sprinted on to pick up Bridget.

Bridget was gasping for breath as he lifted her from the ground and half-carried, half-dragged her toward the creek. He plunged knee-deep into the water and waded out to the nearest wagon, needing both hands to pull Bridget staggering behind him and to ward off the braying mules blundering against them. She was crying for him to slow, to let her regain her balance. But this wasn't the time or place for niceties, bullets whistling over and around and plunking in little geysers into the water alongside. In a kind of modified lifesaver's hold and feedsack toss, Fargo clasped Bridget tightly and boosted her onto the seat, his fling propelling her on through the flap and toppling, wailing, down among the cargo.

Fargo waded toward the bank, ignoring the screeches and crashes coming from the wagon bed behind him. More shots were whining and snapping about, though the riders couldn't aim effectively from pitching saddles behind their smoke screen, and their bullets were off target. But there was a helluva lot of slugs flying around, and luck can last only so long.

Reaching the bank, Fargo sprinted toward Quinelle to retrieve his Sharps, the steady roar of flames drowning the shouts of men and the screams of mules, and the roiling smoke choking them silent. Inadvertently he bumped into Enoch Welch. The oldest of the skinners, a grizzled whang-hide with the predatory face of a timber lobo, he had a vulture's curved beak for a nose and a gashlike mouth under an awning of a gray mustache. And now, Fargo noticed as Welch shoved past, he had the fixed, blank eyes of a man who'd gone berserk.

"We're goners!" Welch lunged dementedly, head down, hands out, for the fire. Fargo charged after him straight into the flames. Welch turned, struck at him with his carbine, which Fargo readily dodged, clamping his hands on the barrel and yanking hard, ripping the weapon out of Welch's grasp. Fargo returned it to Welch butt-first in the brisket, gathered up the gagging man, and led him back.

"Damn wildcat," Fargo declared, depositing Welch by Quinelle. "Tasted blood and launched a single-handed attack right at them."

"I saw him rip off." Quinelle grinned. "Jeez, Enoch, you got balls. Tearin' into 'em don't take brains, just a whole lotta balls."

Welch was slumped panting, speechless. His eyes had calmed and were looking normal now. He nodded gratefully at Fargo.

Fargo returned the carbine, then took his Sharps from Quinelle, saying, "The men're too scattered. We need to line along creek's edge, to cover one another and the wagons, and to give those bastards all they ask for if—when—they bust through the fire."

They split up, Fargo to the left, Quinelle and Welch to the right. Ducking bullets in zigzagging sprints along the bank, Fargo went from man to man as quickly as possible, feeling time was running short, while in his wake the men cautiously moved toward the creek and the main bulk of wagons. Only Henri the Canuck's wagon was not in the water, one wheel having bogged down in a muddy sump on the bank, where it remained stuck until the mules could pull it free. The crew, Fargo thought, should take pride in having rescued sixteen out of the seventeen wagons, and it was possible the flames wouldn't reach Henri's freighter, for the ground there was gumbo that couldn't support more than a very short, sparse weedy cover.

"Here they come," Brea yelled. "Piss on 'em, boys!"

The skinners were stretched out along the bank, weapons ready. Swarming toward them from behind the flames were thirty, maybe forty riders—a horseback mob, by any count. And now Fargo could discern they were white men, of a breed he knew only too well: vicious, gun-hung, furtive watchfulness on lank, stubbled faces, earning their keep by cruelty and violence. He thought he caught a glimpse of the brush-gunner Devin Reed, but he couldn't be sure. He was positive, however, they all hadn't been out at Devin's camp that night he plowed through it. Not surprising; the trek from, say, Fort Laramie was much quicker for a saddle horse than a freight wagon, and these men could sit home and light out on short notice, whenever they were needed.

The Regina teamsters opened fire as the attackers spurred into the intervening curtain of flames and smoke. A half-dozen saddles emptied, yet it hardly seemed to make a dent in the oncoming horde. The teamsters loosened another volley, chambering and triggering in a frantic daze, faces smeared with blood and grit, and soot adding to their ghastly masks. They were stunned by the

73

overwhelming odds against them, frightened by the advancing blaze, the fuming smoke, and blistering heat. They had good reason to be scared, yet as scared as they were, not one of them broke ranks from that line.

Instead, they continued their ragged barrages, digging in low to avoid the withering salvos directed at them. The riders were suffering the brunt of the battle, their sheer numbers raising the chances of a random bullet hitting someone somewhere. And quite a few of their mounts balked at crossing the fireline, shying or halting, leaving their riders perched like sitting ducks. Down they went, stone-dead or wounded, lurching and howling and even burning. The sight and rate of casualties took a lot of steam out of the gunmen's charge, many of them slowing, some tugging rein, none wishing to be a hero.

There was no slackening of the wildfire, however. It stormed down through the shorter grass of the bank toward the creek, encircling Henri the Canuck's freighter, and though continuously threatening with high-laving flames, the blaze could not kindle the meager, sodden growth in between. It roiled on voraciously to very near the water, and the mushrooming smoke choked and blinded the line of defenders. They were forced to retreat, their shouts and curses lost in splashing water, sizzling in the hissing flames.

Coughing and gasping for breath, Fargo averted his face for a moment. Two riders were spurring through the fire when he faced around again, and swiftly he shot twice at the nearer man, who slipped from the saddle and dropped, screaming, into the charred embers.

The second rider galloped directly at him, revolver blasting. Fargo felt one slug pluck at his jacket as he leveled and shot, and he saw the horse stumble to its knees, catapulting the rider over its head. Tiny Quinelle grabbed the rider within a second of his landing, hoisted him under arm, and rushed into the creek. Fargo heard the rider's gurgling gasp. When Quinelle came back, he was alone.

For a while longer, combat raged furiously. Gunmen charged, and Regina bullets, crying in a steady whine, sent them packing back to a respectful distance. Time and again it appeared as if the teamsters were on the road to hell, as flying wedges of horsemen would breach water's edge. And time and again Fargo and the skinners lay waste of them in point-blank, sometimes hand-to-hand clashes. The gunmen, as callous and vicious as they were, still had hopes and promised wages to live for; the outfit they were up against had nothing save inflamed desperation. And the odds had evened mightily before long, the attackers having suffered a fierce toll. Dead men lay on the bank, in the creek, around the ever-moving fire. Empty shells littered everywhere, crunching underfoot.

The attackers began to retreat, drawing away from the bank and ceasing their attempts to overrun the creek. They continued hazing with heavy fire, but increasingly they were turning their horses northward. Their withdrawal built momentum until the last pack of them were galloping out across the plains, vanishing from sight.

A silence descended—a dry, sucked-out, momentary silence.

Then Enoch Welch broke the hush, laughing with shaky relief. "They're runnin'! We stood 'em off, we did!"

"Not so fast," Carajou said. "They're racin' back."

The approaching sound of a fast-pounding horse, however, was coming from up along the creek.

"Don't shoot, *amigos*," the rider yelled as he moved into view.

It was Velázquez, minus his hat and his undershirt, and his hair was scorched to a wiry bristle. But he was grinning toothily, and when Fargo asked him how the cavvy had fared, Velázquez broadened his grin. "All safe, but a little wet."

"M' wagon is not," Henri the Canuck suddenly cried, pointing toward his freighter. "*Foutre!* I need a lot of wet."

Capriciously, a bit of smoldering grass or a wind-flung spark had ignited the canvas cover of the wagon. It spread fast. One moment the cover had a tiny burn hole; the next moment the cover was engulfed in flames, roasting the cargo and beginning to lick at the wagon bed. Skinners tore the burning canvas from the load and beat out the flames with wet blankets, coughing as smoke rasped their throats.

Within minutes this fire was under control. By then, many of the other drivers were keeping watch on their wagons, alert for each spark. The big prairie fire remained ablaze, seemingly stalling all along the north bank until it jumped Bear Creek or the wind shifted, or it burned itself out. Already it was weakening, though it was still gravely menacing, spewing fiery scraps over the creek and wagons, where the men sloshed about, swatting the embers with their blankets.

They groaned and groused, for the gun fray left them aching with innumerable scratches, contusions, nicks, and bruises. It also caused some sprains and chipped bones and minor bullet creases. But they had suffered no deaths, and only two serious injuries. Brea had his left ear shot clean off, and a skinner named Packard had a flesh wound through his left thigh.

Fargo helped carry Packard to a flat, sheltered nook. Sweat rivuleted in streaks down the smear of soot on his face. His hands were equally black, his arms and shoulders and chest were red raw, and he had his share of cuts and lumps, none worth bothering about.

With them was the outfit's *medico*, Upwind Muldoon. He'd never been schooled, but had a knack for doctoring that well made up for his flatulent pastries. The man treated Packard with more skill than many a doctor Fargo had seen. He was sewing Brea's ear back on when Fargo began wading out to the wagon in which Bridget was crouching.

The stymied prairie fire was sputtering low when Fargo reached the wagon, but the acrid smoke still hung like a sulfurous fog. Bridget, on the wagon-box seat, coughed several times before speaking.

"I'm amazed. Has anything, anybody, been hurt or lost?"

"We all hurt, two sorely, but no losses. One canvas gone, one wagon and load slightly scorched, and some mules are down." He smiled casually. "You're down next. Here, give me your hand."

"I prefer not." Gathering her damp, soiled dress, Bridget climbed over the front and, stretching, stepped across to stand on the front wheel. Fargo, watching, had to admit she didn't need his help to get down, for she moved with the assured grace of a supple, long-limbed woman who'd teethed on freighters. Yet even she slid and wavered on the wheel, its iron rim slick from ash and water. She glanced down at the wheel hub, her next and last step to the creek, then looked at Fargo standing close by. She hesitated, reticent.

By the diminishing glow of the fire behind him, Fargo could see anxiety etched on Bridget's face. She was troubled, and he suspected it ran deeper than the happenings here. Yet she hadn't lost the spunk to fight, and now he wondered if her chilly, prudish manner weren't mostly a defense, a shell she threw around herself to keep any weaknesses from showing.

"It was very clever," Bridget said quietly. "Thank you. I—I appreciate how you anticipated and planned and handled things."

"No need. You should expect me to know my work, and to do it."

"I've expected other ... doings from you." Bridget glanced now at the toes of her boots peeking from under her dress, teetered, recaught her balance, and said, "Mr. Fargo, I owe you an apology."

"Give the devil his due?"

"I don't favor your ilk and won't trick you into thinking I do. Still, I was wrong about the chains, the grass, I'm not sure what all, but I was wrong to argue against your orders, period. If I'd won, if you'd heeded me, we'd likely all be dead and Father would be ruined."

Fargo shrugged.

Bridget fell. The rim was slippery, as if greased, and as soon as she moved, her feet whipped out from beneath her. Wobbling, windmilling, she toppled off the wheel. Fargo, springing to catch her, flung out his arms. Bridget let out a startled gasp as her plunge abruptly ended against his chest. Caught by his embracing arms, she wrapped her arms around him reflexively, clinging, hugging.

"I got you," he said, steadying her. "Are you okay?"

Bridget looked up at him, nodding breathlessly.

Fargo met her gaze. For a moment they remained locked together, unmoving, unspeaking. Then, without thinking, Fargo answered an impulse and kissed Bridget tenderly, full on the lips. He didn't know whether it came from some obscure desire to comfort her, or a simple urge to bed the feisty wench, or something else. He didn't care.

Bridget was limp and submissive in his arms, and her mouth was warm against his lips. For a moment, just a moment, she returned his kiss.

Then, wrenching frantically, she broke away and staggered back a pace in the water, gasping, staring. And slapped his face, hard.

Fargo swayed, almost tripping into the water. By the time he recovered, Bridget was already forging toward the bank like a steaming dreadnought. He felt no vast desire to try catching up with her, so he waded to shore at a slightly slower clip, rubbing his cheek.

At one point, he stopped and laughed like hell.

The fire was dying down and the breeze was too. The danger, except for an occasional spark, was over. The teamsters began turning their attention from the wagons to the mules, and Fargo pitched in with readying the gear and mules for hitch-up. Just before dawn, he straightened to ease his aching back, and saw Enoch Welch standing nearby, grimacing with heat-cracked lips.

"Capt'n, you come near dyin' to let me live," Welch said painfully. "Lied for me, to boot, so I could go kill galoots afterward. I dunno why we lived and them died or nuthin'. I made an awful mess of things. I dunno why I'm alive, I ain't deservin'."

"If you ask me," Fargo replied, "it's a deep subject. You only die once, and don't know it after. Why think about it?"

"I tell you what I think about," Henri spoke up, scowling. "Chadwick was behind the raid, I think, yet *le cul* still lives."

"Yep, an' Chadwick will strike again afore long," Quinelle said, joining in. "I didn't see anymany Consolidated teamsters in the rumpus, an' I sorta reckon Chadwick don't mix too many o' them with his down-an'-dirty boys. Can be bad for business. But he'll add his full Consolidated force, if that's what'll take to stomp us."

"Well, let 'em come an' try! We'll be ready for Chadwick, whatever he throws at us," Tobac declared. He was the only one who had come through the raid utterly unscathed. But like all the rest, his expression was a mixture of pride and anger, his dark eyes seething vengefully. "I'm hoping the next time Chadwick shows in person. Then, Henri, you can stop thinking again."

The mild jab earned a ripple of laughter.

Fargo felt pleased about his crew overall—they'd passed the test. They'd beaten the odds and, more important, they'd conquered their worst enemies—themselves—in the process.

In their moment of reckoning, they'd reckoned well.

6

Double teams of mules were hitched to the wagons and they were drawn out on the south bank of Bear Creek. Upwind Muldoon cooked breakfast while the crew reformed the train, and as pale streamers of light brightened the eastern sky, the outfit set off rolling southward again.

During the midmorning break, Fargo left the train as usual to scout the region. A mile out on his western swing, he suddenly reined in. Ahead and around, the grassy plain was flattened and churned by a wide trail of hoofmarks. He moved forward, dismounted, and picked up a tuft of feather, then carefully scrutinized the spots where the riders had blazed a path across open soil. It quickly became apparent that they had been loping south on unshod horses. Unshod horses meant Indian horses.

Fargo walked the trail in an outward-spiraling pattern. He found no sign of shod hooves mingling with the prints, indicating there were no white

men along, such as gun-runners or whiskey ped-
dlers or outlaw cahooters. By the width and track-
plowed nature of the trail, Fargo estimated an
easy hundred, perhaps two hundred riders—
certainly more than any foraging and hunting
group, but the right size for a war party. The
mashed grasses, turned earth, occasional dung
lumps, and splashes of urine all showed a fresh-
ness that put the trail between six to twelve hours
old.

Grimly Fargo continued his inspection for a
short while longer, then returned to the outfit and
informed the men of his findings.

"Sioux," Henri the Canuck said, nodding. "But
maybe not a war party. This time of year they go
cuttin' lodgepoles near the mountains, so maybe
that was a camp of 'em, with women and children."

"Yeah, an' those o' you along on our last train
know them's weren't no Injuns who hit us,"
Quinelle said. "Sorta fits in with the talk of Sioux
warpathin' that all seems to come from Consolidated. Could be just crap, and they ain't interested in fightin' us whites."

Brea laughed scoffingly. "Hell, nobody kin ever
tell when an Indian is fightin' or not fightin'.
Ain't that true, Capt'n?"

"Nobody can who fools himself blind," Fargo
replied brusquely. He doubted Brea believed his
own words or that Henri and Quinelle were as
sanguine as they sounded. They were whistling
past the graveyard, alarmed and worried, just like
everyone else. "Sign was of riders at a lope, which
is too fast for a camp, but slow for a party going on
a raid. Returning from one, possibly, like swiping
Arapaho horses. Whatever, the party came

through just before the fire, or cut in from the west to look it over, and I'd rather we miss looking them over in turn."

"You think they'll attack us?" Carajou asked.

Fargo shrugged. "Best I know, the Sioux aren't in open war. We've got stuff they'd like to have, though, and their parties usually sport lots of young bucks who're spoiling for a fight—any fight."

"But like you say, boss, they're headin' south in front o' us," Welch countered hopefully. "Faster, too. So long's they are, we ain't gonna run into 'em, might ne'er even lay eyeballs on 'em."

"They'll see us, Enoch. They'll soon know we're here, if not already," Fargo said, sensing the men's dread and tightening nerves. "One of their hunters is bound to strike our trail, and they'll come to check us unawares, and they'll leave us unawares if they don't want to bother with us. If they do, they'll show. From a beg for flour to an ambushing raid, when we see them is when we got them, so I just as soon not see them at all."

Thereafter they kept anxious watch, and at noon Fargo scouted long and deep. He located the Indian trail again, but it merely confirmed his feeling that the war party had continued loping south. Otherwise, no trace of anyone, red or white, was spotted then or later as they rolled on. For the prairie was deceptive—appearing to be a flat blank sheet, it was actually a shrouded thicket harboring concealment down in its heat-wavy grasses or in the gullies and burrows of its eroded drypan.

In the early afternoon they forded the thin, dusty green ribbon of Horse Creek. The far western border remained a spine of foothills, more straight now, resembling jumbled steps up to the rugged eastern flanks of the Laramie Range beyond. Fargo still guided the outfit, keeping them more or less parallel with this mountainous chain. Along about midafternoon, they began to pass a series of hogback knolls that rose, like bunched rocky knuckles, from the flats between them and the hills.

The wearied mules were flagging, their break overdue. Fargo scanned the plain and knolls, espying nothing suspicious, yet feeling reluctant to rest hereabouts. It was the knolls, he sensed; he mistrusted such high points and warily avoided lingering under their view. He watched the freighters drawing by the midpoint of the knolls, thinking they'd stop after they'd gone past altogether.

Suddenly the knolls sprouted with Indians, a crowded phalanx of riders suddenly looming along the parched and encrusted linkage of rimline.

"Circle! Go alternate!" Fargo spurred his Ovaro, galloping down one side of the train and up the other. "Alternate circling!"

Popping whips, ranting and raving, the teamsters launched the train circling the way Fargo had taught them earlier on the trail. Carajou swung the lead wagon right, Quinelle turned the second left, the following drivers similarly alternating until they'd formed a circle, then they closed up the wagons so the tongue of one overlapped the wheels of the next in line. Fargo learned this quick method from top-skilled, experienced bullwhackers, who'd corral with oxen faster than others using horses. What the Regina skinners lacked in ability, practice, and spirited teams, they made up for with impetuous gusto inspired by the Sioux, and they corralled the train in half their normal time.

For that Fargo was thankful. He knew the Sioux were more set in their ways than most tribes, and from experience he judged the war party's show was their way to threaten, to frighten, rather than to muster for a sudden surprise attack. Still, he didn't care to risk more than necessary and was relieved the teamsters got as far as chaining the wheels when the Sioux tore down on them. They scrambled up on their wagons, snatching pistols and ammo from under seats and boards, and yanking carbines out of scabbards and slings that were customarily kept on the near side of the wagons, handy to the driver.

"Don't anyone fire," Fargo ordered, dismounting. "Let them see your guns, that we're ready to fight, but don't threaten them."

"You fuckin' crazy, boss? Look at 'em whoopin' and hollerin' a-stormin' to massa-cree us," Tobac yelled, lying under his wagon.

Carajou gave a loud, sarcastic laugh. "That's why they carry on, so you'll think so and scare you pissless. They ain't on no scalp raid, 'cause that's when you don't see or hear 'em, but if any of us rattle now and pop any of 'em, we'll get our raid and lotsa noise."

"Right. Nobody shoots unless I give the word," Fargo insisted. "Can anyone here speak Siouan? No? How about sign lingo?"

"I know some," Brea called. He slid from his

wagon, put his carbine on the seat, and said, "Maybe I'll remember a few cusses."

There were about a hundred and fifty in the party, now racing down and across from the knolls, shouting shrilly, firing early-issue Springfields and Spencers into the air. Fargo went over to Carajou's wagon with Brea a pace behind, making sure Bridget Delahay was safely out of sight in the wagon bed—against her vehement protests. Bridget aquiesced only after Brea agreed she could shoot as well as a man, arguing that she would tempt the bucks to attack when they mightn't otherwise, thus endangering the crew if she didn't stay hidden. Carajou's threat to rope and toss her inside was also a persuader.

Fargo waited within the corral, gazing between two wagons while the war party slowed and began milling about some hundred yards away. For a moment or two after leaving Bridget, however, he wondered about her behavior. She'd avoided him since the fire, but she wasn't the first woman to snub him or call him disreputable and dishonorable, and such guff generally didn't bother him unless it interfered with work. Now it was. The outfit lived on teamwork, needing everyone to pull together, yet Bridget had become distant, riding horseback rather than with the drivers, civilly yet coolly shunning all company. Teamsters don't suffer rejection well, and if her cuts worsened, they could split the outfit.

Brea, standing alongside Fargo, broke into his thoughts. "You ne'er learned Injun palaver, eh? Huh, I'd've bet you knowed, Capt'n."

"I do more or less, depending on the tribe." Fargo smiled at Brea, who was a faceful of whiskers between a battered brown hat and a blue flannel shirt, with dark pants tucked into bowie-sheathed legging boots. He was biggest after Quinelle and, Fargo estimated, next to Henri in skill with whips, able to flick ash from a cigarette at twenty paces, or to throttle a man. "Brea, one Sioux ploy is for the head chieftain to talk only through someone lesser, like he can't stoop to our low level. If I'm our chief and talk, we lose more status and bargaining power. We pull the same stunt by talking through you—we win some."

"Yah, we'll snoot them." Brea belly-laughed. "I used to speak so-so Algonquin, and they're the ones who named the Sioux. Means 'snake-like-one,' 'cause of their crafty ways." When he saw Fargo's expression of interest, Brea grinned sheepishly. "I, ah, was a squaw man, y'see. M'wife was Algonquin. She died."

"Sorry."

A half-dozen Sioux rode forward slowly, hands upraised.

Brea swore. "Too many young bucks. I don't like it."

"Don't forget, consult me on everything," Fargo reminded him, propping his Sharps against a wheel and climbing between the two wagons. Approaching, he studied the six ahead and briefly surveyed the party mobbed a ways behind. Tall, sinewy, hawk-nosed, the Sioux were resplendent in gaudy war clothes, with brightly painted shields and lances, their spotted Indian ponies painted with the same material the braves had daubed on their faces.

Brea spoke to them in sign language. Three of the Sioux chieftains were older men, and three fell into Brea's young-buck category; one of the elders displayed a haughty disdain that stamped him as the head. Well, it was supposed to, Fargo thought wryly—their whole act was to impress and intimidate as leverage when bargaining.

"Red men wish to greet white brothers," Brea reported, grinned. "Think o' that! I see whatcha mean about the snob."

"Ignore him. He's beneath us. Ask them what they want."

"Presents, what else?"

Fargo saw the chieftains staring at the wagons. He called to Quinelle inside the corral, "Bring out three bags of flour, a sack of sugar, and a drum of molasses."

While Carajou and Upwind Muldoon helped Quinelle carry the goods out and place them on the ground, Fargo and Brea continued to negotiate with the chieftains. What with all the relaying and discussing, the parlay was a slow and desultory haggle over how much the train could be shaken down for.

"More," Brea repeated groggily as the three teamsters returned to the wagons. "They're saying again it ain't enough."

"This is tantamount to a water-drip torture," Fargo grumbled. "It's all they're going to get. Tell them the rest is all army supplies going to the bluebellies at Crow River."

Brea told, and their reply, "Loosely translated, bullshit."

"Tell them . . . No. Take one of the older chieftains, not the head, and show him Packard's and Jewett's wagons. They're all army."

Silence descended during the brief lull while

Brea and the chieftain were gone. Fargo turned his back to the others and kept his back to them after the chieftain returned with Brea, waiting till the Sioux finished their powwow before instructing Brea.

"Tell them to take what they got. If they make a stab at the wagons, they'll just get army stuff and the army after them, and if they give us more argument now, *we'll* get the army after them."

Brea chuckled. "That's the language they understand, Capt'n."

The Sioux finally picked up their tribute and rode back with it.

Fargo watched the entire war party whirl southward, remarking to Brea, "Closer than I care for. I missed a lot—they were arguing too fast—but I caught their jist. The bucks aren't satisfied, aren't scared of the army because they don't give a damn who they fight, their guts haven't shriveled. The older chiefs told them they're too young to know their pricks from twigs, or they'd know caution isn't fear but smarts, and another piece of smarts is to take what was given them."

Brea sighed. "You figure they'll come back?"

"They will if someone brings them," Fargo replied sagely.

"Y'know," Brea said, "I wouldn't put it past Chadwick . . ."

Shortly the teams were rehitched, a final check made of the gear, and Fargo shouted the wagon captain's traditional command: "Stretch 'em out!" The outfit moved from the treacherous knolls at an easy gait, wanting to conserve the draining strength of their weary mules. For even after water, feed, and an albeit shortened break period, the poor gluefoots were fatigued from the lengthy days.

The broiling sun sharpened its angle as it descended into late afternoon. Its arcing slant through a cloudless azure sky created a strange optical illusion across the plain, transmuting the shimmery waves of grass to bright stone and glittery sand, blindingly reflective. Fargo was estimating there might be two, three hours before twilight, when he straightened in the saddle and glimpsed ahead another seeming mirage, an oddity called Council Crest.

Council Crest was no crest at all, but a pie-shaped wedge much longer than it was tall, stretching, as the knolls had, up from the flatland out of nowhere. It had been, Fargo once heard, a buckled land plate warped by some prehistoric earthquake; it was also a freak of the water table, being not only a prairie tank—a rarity in itself— but an artesian spring as well. The water tasted gawd-awful, supposedly the result of too much alkali, but the one time Fargo had tried a taste of it, he thought it was from rotten-egg sulfur.

Nobody knew or could remember where the "Crest" originated. It just always was. The "Council" was easy to surmise, likely dating back to when Indian tribal meetings were held there, for it had never been other than a popular gathering place. It was covered with groves and copses and a few thick stands of timber—hardwood trees sprouting where few or no trees grew.

It was at Council Crest, in a wide, scalloped indentation along the shallow base of the hill, that the outfit corralled for the night. Within an hour they had pitched cook fire and camp, and had the mules grazing out on the plain a mile away. Fargo sent half the crew with axes up into the woods to search for hickory groves. Regularly—chronically—the Regina wagons had been threatening to fall apart, axles and wheels snapping across the eroded drypan. Here they would replenish the spare axles they'd already used up.

With time came deepening shadows, and through the hazy purple dusk rode Fargo, scouting for signs of the war party. He returned after dark, having found none, yet unconvinced the Sioux had given up for good. They might have a change of mind at any time, so as an added precaution, he took his bedroll up Council Crest to a good vantage point and settled, watching, listening, for the night.

His lookout was among a low nest of boulders above the small but very deep tank. The pale crescent of moon and sprinkling of stars cast scarcely any light at all, and the prairie vastness remained swathed in gloom, indistinct and dimensionless. Silent.

Presently the faint pad of footsteps carried up to him. He turned in the direction of the sound, hearing and then seeing a dark figure approaching the tank. He wasn't absolutely sure of its identity until it crossed the strip of gravel to the water's edge and started taking off a dress. He called out, "No bathing, Bridget."

She gasped, startled, staring about. "Skye? That you?"

"Up here." He wondered if she realized she'd used his first name.

"You gave me some fright. And, and thanks for being decent enough to warn me. Now, if you'll turn your back, I'd like to slip off my clothes and change into something wet."

"Bridget, you can't swim in the tank," Fargo explained, "for the same reason animals who're natural enemies instinctively don't fight around it. Contamination."

"Have you had a drink of it? That water's already poisonous," she countered, climbing toward him. A moment later she eased in among the rocks, and Fargo made room for her to sit down on his bedroll. "My, this's like a little watchtower," she remarked. "Very private."

"That's the idea. I see you, you can't see me." Fargo lapsed silent for a long stretch then, his senses attuned to the surroundings.

Bridget suddenly asked, "You were thinking about me?"

"No," he replied, and it was true, he hadn't been.

Bridget didn't believe him. "Yes, you were. You're angry with me for slapping you, probably blame me for leading you on, don't you?"

When Fargo didn't answer, Bridget lowered her head and murmured, "It's so easy for you men to do what you please. A girl can't get away with it, believe you me. I wasn't allowed to do anything, especially after Mom died. Dad wouldn't allow me to go to dances, meet boys, nothing! It's all so black and white, either saloon-girl whore or respectable lady. Who wouldn't get sick of it? I ran off, married a gambler named Lloyd, mostly to spite my dad."

Fargo shifted slightly, uncomfortable around intimate confessions. "You don't have to say more."

She shook her head, and her voice had a hitch in it now. "Oh, those were the days. Lloyd got me interested in gambling, too. The faro, the drinking, the fancy clothes and fine restaurants when we had money, and . . ." She sobbed softly, leaning against Fargo's arm. "I became a greedy shrew. Lloyd lost his respect, I suppose, or found a new love, but in any case he dumped me in St. Louis. I came home vowing never again, but oh, I did adore the life so. Even when I knew it was wicked, Skye, even when I knew!"

Against his better judgment, Fargo held her and stroked her back as he might have a distraught child. Yet Bridget was not a child; she was very much a woman, who cried for her lost virtue. He thought of how she pictured herself, an avaricious wanton reveling in sin, deserving to be abandoned. There was nothing sweet or charming about that image . . . but then, there was nothing sweet and charming about lust, either, and his loins were beginning to throb with crude desire.

Perversely Bridget pressed against him, close. Her breathing grew stronger, heavier. She glanced up and seemed to sense intuitively what was stirring within him. She plucked lightly at his jacket. "I've tried to resist. I've fought when I'd weaken, and I've done both on this trip. It's been so hard, Skye, so long . . ."

"It sure has," Fargo muttered under his breath. He could feel her body trembling as she stretched and their lips met, as if surges of forbidden delight were pulsing in response to his hunger.

Bridget pulled away, gasping, and surveyed his lean, angular body with yearning eyes. "Do you love me, Skye?" she whispered, trembling. "I hope you don't say you do. I don't want that tonight."

"No, Bridget. No, we're strangers, really. No love."

"Good. I know as soon as we get back, I'll be the proper woman again. But just once, Skye, I want something to regret in the morning."

She was standing now, unfastening her dress. Gracefully she slid it over her head, then removed her boots and string-tied lacy drawers. Fargo's eyes gazed at her pale white thighs, almost phosphorescent against the ebony landscape, and the soft, curly thatch between her legs. She radiated heat and light . . . and passion.

"We'll remain strangers, Skye. But you've been wanting me, and your wanting has made me want you. Lord, I've missed being wanted."

Timidly naked she stood, still somewhat shocked by her own boldness. She was trembling, her luxuriant hair falling across shoulders as smooth as satin. Her long, svelte legs were parted and quivered gently with the tremulousness of a shy animal. And in that posture, her firm, globular breasts with their golden-brown nipples were swaying ever so gently, as though visibly palpitating from fear of being suddenly attacked and devoured.

Grabbing her wrist, Fargo drew her to his bedroll. As she settled close to him, his lips mashed against hers, parting them, his tongue searching her mouth like a fiery salamander. She encircled him with her arms around his neck, running her hands through his black hair, then his beard, then down his shirtfront to his groin, gripping through his trousers and playfully squeezing.

"I've always wanted to do this to a man," she sighed between kisses. "Naughty, naughty, mustn't touch!"

"You mean that Lloyd . . . ?"

"Lloyd's love was gambling."

Fargo felt her other hand glide down now and begin unbuckling his belt. He lifted to his knees to give her room as her urgent fingers quickly thrust his pants down around his thighs. "So hard, so marvelously hard," she crooned, looking down to watch her hands rub and fondle him, her lips slack and wet, a haunted expression in her eyes. "I don't love you. I love this, though . . ."

Fargo gripped her roughly, his needs hot and flowing. Their bodies met and melded together, their lips and loins rubbing and pressing greedily while Fargo undressed, the interruptions constant yet pleasant. He felt the pressure of their bellies against each other, and the throbbing pulse of his flesh lancing against her loins, and her moistly gripping crevice widening for him.

In her ecstatic haste, she squirmed to spread herself beneath him. But Fargo grinned down at her, clutched her around the waist, and lifted her up over him. "It's your night to howl, so you set the pace," he urged.

"Oh, I can't, I never . . ." Her protest trailed off into a little crooning hum as Fargo's hands guided her into a kneeling position over his body. "I feel so depraved, Skye, so utterly debauched."

She wriggled in an odd mixture of trepidation and desire, gripping the sides of his chest with her knees. Gingerly she reached down and aimed him toward her pink cleft while she gradually settled lower into a squatting position.

"Ahhh, you feel so long," she sighed, hesitating.

"There's more if you want it," he replied, feeling himself rigid and thick as he slid deeper inside her.

"I want it all," he heard her gasp when she bent forward to kiss him. "I said I'm greedy."

Greedy she was. Insatiable. Fargo had no idea what on earth this Lloyd jerk must have been thinking when he confined a naturally lusty female like Bridget to only missionary-position puritanical sex. It was incredible to Fargo that any woman as vivacious and passionate as the one bucking above him would not have been taken this and every other which way, but he was now delighting in the consequences. The novelty of riding a man and controlling the motion seemed to thrill her, mingling shame and pleasure.

Fargo also realized that it must have taken considerable daring on her part to strip naked out in the middle of a forlorn hill, while her Regina crew was corralled a short distance away. And now to be writhing, heaving, gasping, thrashing, with just his hard shaft connecting them, made the entire act even more shocking and exciting. She moaned deliriously and pushed herself down upon him even harder, hoping to impale herself further. And in turn, her frenzy was making Fargo feel surrounded, engulfed in her mania for self-fulfillment and expression.

Bridget began increasing the length and tempo of her thrusts, bracing herself on her arms and knees, pushing and retreating, pushing and retreating. Her rhythm increased as her orgasm approached. In a short moment she was rearing skyward until Fargo was almost totally exposed, then she was plunging down all the way, violently, as he surged into her depths like a white-hot bludgeon, setting her afire inside.

It hit Bridget first. She whimpered and sobbed; then, as her orgasm erupted, she bit down on her lower lip to keep from screaming. She reared and plunged madly, grinding herself against him, digging her fingers into his arms, her face and neck flushed with blood, her eyes glazed with satisfaction.

Watching her, Fargo felt himself stiffen and become larger within her. He let out a long, delicious sigh as he felt his release fountain up in hot jets into her seething belly. . . .

They went limp. Bridget lay on him and crooned softly. "I don't believe I'll regret this tomorrow. I don't think I'm going back to being a proper lady. I think I have misspent my youth and will have to make arrangements so I can make up for lost time."

Fargo stretched back on the bedroll and grinned up at her. "Give me a few minutes, and I'll rearrange you."

She gasped. "There are other ways of doing it?"

"This may be a long night," Fargo whispered.

It was.

7

The outfit got away to an early start in the gray of a new dawn. With eyes haggard and bloodshot from loss of sleep, Fargo tried to keep a sharp watch for possible trouble as shadows still clung to pockets and dry washes and the horizon slowly brightened. Nor did he relax with the garish sheen of daylight. Again, as on the previous afternoon, he sensed eyes were on him, on the train; he surveyed constantly, spotting nothing, yet remaining chary.

Once when riding by the lead wagon, he drew alongside and shifted irritably in his saddle, remarking, "We're being watched."

Carajou peered about. "Yeah? Where?"

"In the air, underfoot, damned if I know. Keep an extra keen lookout today, though, will you? And your carbine across your lap."

"Sure." Carajou thumbed toward Bridget, who'd returned to accompany him on the wagon seat. " 'Course, I'll let my shotgunner handle the gun-totin' duties, now that she's back to feelin' chipper."

Fargo glanced sidelong at Bridget. "You were sick?"

"Nursing a spell of broods, Mr. Fargo, in case you hadn't noticed. But fully recovered, veritably overnight, and flowing with the milk of human, ah, kindness."

Later, however, Bridget confided to Fargo, "The main reason I wanted to wagon-ride is that I've got a sore fanny."

As the sun continued to rise, so did Fargo's edginess. It was not until the sun was just past its zenith that he discovered the slightest trace of anything amiss, when a remote movement to the southwest caught his attention. A hawk was spiraling lower between two foothill ridges, only to soar high again as if unsettled.

Focusing intently, the Trailsman scrutinized the hawk's lazy, predatory circling against the backdrop of shimmery crags, and he glimpsed a rising trickle of smoke. It was such a vague gossamer thread that it was barely discernible; that it came from a campfire, Fargo had no doubt, but whose and why made him curious. When time came for the midafternoon break and wisping smoke was still visible, he pointed it out to the crew, saying, "You'll have to squint hard to see it. That we can at all is one of the things that bothers me."

"I'd worry about more, like from a grass fire," Packard said.

"Or seein' it in puffs, like for signaling," Jewett said.

"Yeah, so what?" Welch asked. "It's just a dumb cook fire."

"May be perfectly innocent," Fargo allowed, nodding. "A drover crew or a lone drifter, say, who'd have to be innocent and damnably dumb to call any note to himself out here. And he must be slow-frying a buffalo, because the fire's been burning that way for hours."

"Injuns," Tobac suggested. "That war party."

"Outside of their villages, when have you seen smoke at a distance from a Sioux camp? Never, unless for a reason, such as a signal."

"Then what's it be, Capt'n?" Henri asked.

Fargo shrugged. "It's too far and weak to tell. Keep track of it as we go, so if it changes, if something happens over there, one of us is apt to see it."

Presently the tall grass thinned and shortened to stubbly bear grass as the outfit entered a stretch of poor soil, gravel and loose shale. Soon after that the yonder smoke disappeared altogether. Came evening, and they filed through a sparse grove of cottonwood to emerge on a low, deeply eroded cliff overlooking Lodgepole Creek. The bank below ran on a shallow incline to the water, now seasonally low, a torpid yellow-green. Except for a fringe of briars and interwoven vines, the long bank was dried clay and silt, cracked into curlicue patterns, and not the sort of place to corral the train.

Scouting, Fargo found the other side to be very much the same. But at least it was heading in the right direction, not backtracking through the cottonwood grove, so he led them across where the creek was only about two hundred feet wide and the bottom was sandy and firm. A short ways from the shoreline, they camped in a flat, open field surrounded by a corrugated expanse, pebbled and weedy.

"There's a hunch I want to follow," Fargo then told Brea and Henri the Canuck. "Might do to have company, of a dead-quiet nature."

The men nodded, Henri saying, "My snake flicks a silent tongue."

Putting Quinelle in charge, Fargo ordered preparations in case of an attack. Some precautions were obvious, such as readying firearms, powder, and shot; others needed explanation, such as unloading the six barrels of oil that were part of the freight. When Fargo was satisfied that things were being seen to, he rode out with Brea and Henri on a sly, twisty course toward the area where they'd seen the smoke.

For much of the distance they went upstream along the waterline, keeping below the cliff of the bank and away from the lancing glare of sunset. The terrain began a gradual rise, choppy and broken, Lodgepole Creek flowing roughly between narrowing, steepening sides. The ruggedness of the approaching foothills dulled with encroaching dusk, blurring over and filling in with shadows, shrouding the three riders when they finally quit the creek and angled overland.

Night smoothed the mountainous country further, to a textured ebony as infinite as the blackened sky. Southwest of the creek, the trio at length hiked through a region of fissured slabs and benches sprouting sagebrush and yucca, and of scraggly boxelders clinging to ledges and clefted slopes. They perused their surroundings continuously, ears tuned to catch the weakest noise. They detected what they thought were vague, faint cries drifting on the wind from up ahead, nearly inaudible and lacking clarity or direction.

Eventually they reached the foot of a slope dotted with saltbush and trembling aspen. They paused once again, listening, scrutinizing, convinced they couldn't be too far off from those crags where they'd pinpointed the fire. Sharp as their eyes and ears were, they wouldn't have glimpsed or heard any telltale sign, if first there hadn't been a delicate twist of breeze bringing the fragrant odor of wood smoke. The breeze died, but the single whiff had been sufficient.

"Smells of fresh burnings, not stale smolderings," Fargo said as he dismounted. "Folks are tending that fire. We best go on foot."

"Yeah, I dunno the chances of 'em being Sioux, but I'm takin' no chances on 'em *not* being Sioux," Brea said while they ground-reined their horses. "Sneaky does it. Our cayuses would make too much clatter, and one's yet to be foaled that could belly-crawl."

From their saddle horns Brea and Henri took coiled blacksnakes, each having about an eighteen-inch stock and some thirty feet of braided rawhide lash. Fargo added a couple of sheathed Green River knives, honed and balanced for throwing. They left their rifles, though, figuring they'd more likely be hampered than helped by noisy, cumbersome long guns. They were scouting, after all, not attacking.

Starting up through the clumps of trees and low-growing brush, they eased over the rounded crest of the slope and began to descend the other side. The aroma of smoke grew more distinct, but they remained deaf and blind to its source for almost a quarter-mile of skirting ledges, spanning culverts, and threading boulders and thickets. Then, as they crossed a bench and were nearing its edge, they heard a low murmuring drone with occasional laughs or shouts echoing up very softly into the soundless night. They stopped when they reached the rim, staring below and beyond into a wide, shallow, dished canyon.

The dry bed of a brook or runoff wriggled along one side and out through the apparent mouth of the canyon. From the opposite side bulged a gentle mound of shrubs and copses and, strangely, a smallish one-ton freight wagon, tarp-covered and parked in full view. Its dark outline atop the hillock overlooked a sprawling encampment of Indians. Or rather, an encampment of sprawling Indians. No squaws, no tepees, only Sioux braves chinning and smoking and cleaning a few guns, while they clustered on blankets around tiny fires.

A clearing stretched at the base of the hillside fronting the wagon. Directly across it was a large pocket hemmed in on most of three sides by a row of boulders, like snaggled teeth, but wide open along its fourth side. Braves rose and sauntered through the clearing from time to time, gazing up the hill yet never climbing. Nor did they venture near the pocket, wherein could be glimpsed a lively blaze encircled by blanketed men—the chieftains, no doubt, and their coterie.

"*Merde,*" Henri grumbled as they lay prone at

the rim and studied the camp. "Those 'uns down there are that same war party."

Fargo scowled. "Not all of them. Aren't those whites by the hill? And looks like the chiefs are meeting with Tully Nickles."

"Nickles?" Brea tightened, staring. "Right, his red hair's a giveaway. Must be thirty o' his pals bunched o'er there a-waitin'."

"This explains the smoke. It didn't just happen, like from all them little fires clouding together; those are sized to cook one meal, obviously tonight's, and are lit too late to cause the smoke we saw," Frago surmised aloud. "No, the chieftains burned wet or oily stuff there in the pocket, not by accident, but as a beacon to guide Nickles and his gang here. Afterward they switched to dry, smokeless wood."

"And then? What've they been up to ever since?" Henri asked.

"Dickering, I bet. The Sioux make grand sport of it." Fargo began to slither over the edge. "Maybe I can learn what about."

Brea blurted. "You can't alone, we'll all go—"

"No. Why risk going? You'll know as much as soon as I'm back, and you won't get caught if I am. If I am, leave fast. That's an order."

Grimly, Fargo crept down and around the canyon bank toward the pocket. Crouching behind the paltry cover of each slim rock and twiggy bush, he tensed, alert for any sign that his approach had been detected. He didn't see anything wrong, though the hillock on which the wagon sat aroused his suspicions like the knolls had yesterday. He didn't hear anything wrong, but was unable to make sense of the indistinct mutterings from the pocket, other than to determine they didn't sound alarmed.

Eventually reaching the shoulder of the closest boulder, Fargo paused a cautious moment. Satisfied, he dipped between boulders into a slender crevice, squeezed through to the pocket side, and ducked forward to a kneeling position behind a waist-high wedge of stone.

A dozen men were around the fire. The three older chieftains squatted across from other Sioux who had the look of advisers or satraps or trusted cronies. The younger chieftains sat in between, facing a brown-haired gunman with a scarred upper lip and a smugly relaxing Tully Nickles. Fargo settled in to follow the parlay, still having difficulty understanding the garble of voices. But the Sioux and Nickles had to deal in sign language, and Fargo was positioned where he could read most of their exchange.

It quickly became evident that Nickles was holding out for something that the younger chieftains seemed willing to give, the older chieftains not at all willing. Once Fargo sorted out the details, so little new was being discussed that his mind started to stray. He decided to withdraw and began to wonder about the brush-gunner Devin Reed, who wasn't here or with the furtively watching gunmen bunched nearby. Backing from the boulders, Fargo silently hastened up and over the slope.

"Well?" Brea demanded. "What's the palaver down there?"

"Nickles wants the Sioux to join in attacking our train."

"Mon dieu! When a man goes that far—"

"Nickles will stop at nothing so long's Chadwick pays him to stop at nothing," Fargo declared with a cold laugh. "The two must have met after we routed their grassfire raiders, and Chadwick sent off Nickles with fresh plans and supplies. Orders may have been to contact the Sioux directly and make his pitch. Or they may have been to follow us from afar, ready to take advantage of any break, and Nickles saw his opportunity when we hit the war party. Whichever, if he connives the Sioux into siding with his gang, they'll outnumber us more than ten to one."

Brea shook his head. "Least they're talkin', so they can't've all swallowed his blarney. The older chieftains, they still reckon kicking our butt ain't worth the army stompin' their shit, don't they?"

"Maybe, maybe not. Nickles sweetened the payoff by offering a wagonload of rifles and ammo. That's his wagon on the hill, which he hauled there as a display to whet the Sioux tastebuds, and it exerts a powerful tempting pressure against caution and smarts."

"They'd attack the wagon if it held guns," Henri scoffed.

"Instead, they avoid it, shun the hill, and it's easy to figure why. Some gunmen like Devin Reed must be at the wagon, threatening to blow it up if approached, while probably Nickles is warning the same if his offer is rejected. What other hold do they have on the Sioux?" It was a rhetorical question, and Fargo continued, "If the Sioux refuse, we'll go on as before. Now, I doubt they will; the younger chieftains want those weapons so bad they're chewing their moccasins. If the Sioux accept, we'll be wiped out, likely first of many, plus lots of bloody battles before the load of rifles runs its course."

"What'll we do?" Henri asked, frowning. "What can we do?"

"Get rid of the wagon and then get the hell out."

Brea and Henri didn't question what would be done, what *had* to be done, any more than Fargo had when learning of the arms by sign language. Hiking along the canyon near its crest, they came to a part of the bank that was relatively close above the hillock and profusely studded with boulders and foliage. They slewed down the slope, then slipped along a series of thin, angular ledges. The ledges petered out and they began a slow, difficult descent through the matted grove, every snap of a twig holding danger as they edged lower to the Sioux encampment. There were bound to be some braves watching, Fargo thought as they pushed quietly across a wide perimeter strip of greenery.

The first brave they encountered was half-asleep, taking a leak against a tree. Break knocked him down with a sledgehammering fist, and Henri picked him up and punched him flat cold on his back. They moved on.

Two Indians were talking in gutturals and were dispatched without ceremony. After dragging the bodies deeper into the shrubbery, they hesitated, peering about them. Other than a faint sigh of wind, all was as still as death.

They were about to shift from their spot when Fargo heard something that might have been the wind, but he doubted it. An almost inaudible feathery sound, like a plant brushing a rock. But not likely. Silently he withdrew one of his dagger-point Green River knives, while Brea and Henri unlimbered the blacksnakes, and they wormed single-file around a patch of saltbush, then paused in the crook of two large boulders at the bottom backside of the hillock. Their progress had been gradual and noiseless.

But not quite noiseless enough.

Nor was the attacker noiseless enough, a scuff of moccasins behind and above warning them just in time. Swiveling, they glimpsed a wiry figure, light tan of skin, black of hair and eyes, leaping at Fargo from an outcropping high between the boulders. The diver had his mouth open to yell, and his skinning knife clenched overhead to rip Fargo from face to belly as he plunged past to land.

Still pivoting aside, Fargo parried the slashing knife with a diagonal upthrust of his left forearm while arching his own blade high in a throat-slitting parabola. With the Sioux's windpipe severed, his yell died in a pink spray of blood. But Fargo, as well as Brea and Henri, took little notice, their attention focused on locating the next brave as this one was tumbling limply against the bloody earth.

Apparently the dead Sioux had been a loner, for they discerned no others as they climbed with patient caution. They avoided crossing gravel and loose shale as much as possible, taking advantage of bare ledges and troughlike depressions, parting scraggly undergrowth carefully and slinking through with hardly a sound. Gradually wending higher, they reached a fringe of mountain mahogany growing near the rounded crest. They glided between the trees until, hunkering, they could glance through the slight openings in the limbs.

Fargo was fairly confident they were higher, closer to the wagon, than the Sioux cared to venture. There would only be Chadwick's gunmen, however many Nickles assigned up here—three? four?—including the elusive brush-gunner. Still, it wasn't like clipping off unwary braves. They were hard-case pros, coyote-quick and mean.

Between them and the wagon was a sharp slope, followed by more brush and rock. The stone face of the slope was thankfully short but slippery as grease, forcing them to slither on elbows and knees until they could wedge into the scrub. Ahead loomed a great huddle of conical stones like a tumbled hedgerow. Hidden movement on their far side was barely discernible, but it was enough for Fargo to zero in on, Brea and Henri a pace behind, as they burrowed through the bushy growth and crawled across the rocks, trying to slide between the cracks.

They bellied in from the left and saw the white tarp of the covered freight wagon glimmering in the starlight. The wagon itself was plain and typical, painted a standard red and green, lacking any unique trait that could allow it to be traced back to Chadwick. There were stone chocks under the wheels, and the spark from a man's cigar showed at the front end, up by the doubletree hammer.

Fargo padded out from cover, motioning for Brea and Henri to fan out along the sides in a pinscer movement. He reached the wagon and scouted around one big hind wheel, keeping close to the body. He was leaning forward, low, balancing himself with one hand while clenching his knife in the other, when he ran smack into Devin Reed coming around the front of the wagon.

Fargo clinched, seeking to throttle the brush-gunner. He heard gagging coughs and Reed went limp in his arms, and he reflexively relaxed his hand. Instantly Reed dived backward, thrusting away savagely, hauling up that sawed-off shotgun from inside his long vest.

Tackling low, Fargo tried to grapple the hand holding the brush gun's triggers, fearfully aware that one shot would end it. He twisted, throwing his weight, trying to jam the twin rebounding hammers with the flesh of his wrapping palm. He felt twin stabs of pain as Reed pulled at the triggers.

Countering immediately, Fargo hunched his shoulder, driving it upward. Reed's mouth was open to shout, but the blow struck him in the chin, snapping his jawbone as though it were made of rotten sticks. Fargo's blade went in and twisted, slicing, and Reed went down.

Red droplets were raining from his knife as Fargo heeled around, eyes darting, and glimpsed two more gunmen. They came lumbering in from bordering stands of trees, where apparently they had spread their sugans for sleep. Fargo started running, but the men were spaced too far apart. There wasn't a chance of his making one, much less both men, without someone yelling in alarm.

Suddenly Brea appeared, plunging from the side to intercept. The bullwhip in his hands was leaping and its long lash struck true to the mark with a snap and a pop. The gunman on Fargo's left reeled, jerking, his hands pawing upward for his throat. He stumbled, collapsed, and dropped dead, sprawling forward on his face.

Fargo saw the gunman on his right, mouth

agape, raise his pistol. The neck-whipped man was just going down at that moment, tying up Brea and his blacksnake, and Fargo reckoned Henri was off on the other side, too far away to be of any help. He held his Green River low, on his palm, gauging—then threw upward in a swift motion, without checking his pace.

The knife hurtled through the air and, point first, skewered the throat of the openmouthed gunman. He was knocked backward, working his jaw as if to yell, but incapable of a sound because his windpipe was severed along with his jugular veins, which fountained blood as he crumpled to the ground.

Reaching him, Fargo pulled his knife free and wiped its blade clean on the man's shirt. He started trotting back to the wagon while Brea, recoiling his blacksnake, continued to prowl along that side. There was at least one more gunman to account for, Fargo knew, but as yet there was no sign of him, or of Henri.

The gunman showed himself abruptly, telltale cigar glowing brightly as he launched himself from around the front of the wagon. He was leveling an octagonal-barreled rifle as though bayonet charging to impale Fargo. He had no bayonet, but his finger was squeezing the trigger, and despite Fargo's instant reaction as he lunged at the man, there was no way he could down him before the alarming shot. Afterward the wagon might still be destroyed—but so would he, Brea, and Henri the Canuck.

Braided rawhide sang in the air, then, and like a thin, elongated tentacle wrapped looping about the man's head and neck. He lurched from the constriction, but his momentum kept him upright and plowing forward, the rifle still poised as if to lance Fargo in the gut.

Pivoting aside as the rifle speared past, Fargo snap-kicked the gunman, splintering ribs, collapsing a lung, and traumatizing the heart. The man, his neck cracked and strangling from the lassoing whip, gave a last rattling cough and toppled over, losing his cigar.

Henri came hustling around the same front edge of the wagon, reeling in his whip. "Was almost 'pon him when he made his pounce at you, Capt'n," he said, and shook his head grouchily. "Had to snake quick, at short range, but t'ain't no excuse for givin' that much slack or castin' sloppy around corners. He's it, on my side."

Nodding, Fargo climbed on the wagon and sliced open the tied-down tarpaulin. Filling the entire bed were long wooden boxes of a familiar rectangular shape. "Farm tools, my ass," he muttered, using his thicker-bladed hunting knife to pry up a slat of one box.

He was not surprised by what was packed inside: Spencer rim-fire repeaters of current, military-issue .56-56 caliber, looking well-worn but serviceable. Stacked between the rifle crates were canisters of No. 5 black powder and other, square boxes; Fargo didn't have to open them to know they contained ammunition.

Then Brea approached. Except for his soft boot falls, there was complete silence on the hill, and the only other noise came from restlessly encamped Indians and the pocket where Nickles dealt with the stolid chiefs.

Jumping down, Fargo told Brea and Henri what

he'd in mind, ordering them, "Tear up the canvas tarp and throw some dry brush in the wagon. C'mon, quiet and quick, we've no time to waste."

Hurriedly they ripped the tarp to shreds, then spread out to gather kindling wood. After Fargo rocked the wheels, removing the restraining cobbles with great care, he climbed into the wagon bed and piled the brush in the center of the load. Henri brought a last armful and Brea chuckled. "Gonna roll all over God's heaven," Brea said.

Fargo sparked a sulfur and ignited the dry tinder. He spent a moment nursing the blaze, then opened a canister and dribbled some black powder about, estimating how swiftly the fire would grow.

"Start leaning," he called, low but urgently, dropping to the ground. Brea and Henri set shoulder against the tailgate and shoved. Fargo bent to the wheel of the heavy, fully loaded wagon, thankful he'd picked this ox-strong pair to accompany him.

Slowly the wheels turned over. Fargo ran to the front, grabbed the wagon tongue, and as the teamsters kept thrusting, he struggled to steer the wagon toward the hillside. Progress was snail-paced, but after much straining, the wagon was jockeyed on a collision course with the clearing below and, with luck, the pocket beyond.

Fargo went back to pushing. The wagon dragged in its tracks, and the fire in its bed was crackling now. Any moment a spark or a stray dab of powder could touch off the whole shooting works, but they continued to exert a steady, strong pressure, feeling momentum gradually gather as they began the descent.

Brea said, "Together!"

They all gave one more heave in unison, toes digging the earth, muscles bulging . . . until, abruptly, they went staggering, the wagon trundling away on its own. Catching themselves, they watched it jouncing downhill, increasing speed, its fire brightening from the fanning draft. They left as the rumble of its wheels upon rock grew louder, drawing attention from below. A shout arose, immediately swelling to a chorus of shock and alarm.

Fargo heard the outcry while racing the other way with Brea and Henri. It added impetus to their flight, and they ran, slipping and stumbling, down the hill toward the side of the canyon. They hit bottom, about to plunge into the intervening strip of foliage, when the wagon exploded with a terrific, brilliant shock wave. The bed and crates burst, splintering as flames geysered skyward, and mangled rifles, stone, and dirt cascaded in fiery shrapnel. The concussion was deafening, hurling thick clouds of smoke and debris over the Indians.

Brea stared. "I'd ne'er believed it'd thump that good."

"Save your breath," Fargo snapped. "Run!"

They dived through to the canyon wall, then blazed a path up to the rim and headed straight for their horses. Black powder smoke blanketed the canyon floor, concealing the extent of damage and casualties. But no matter if the wagon had detonated smack in the pocket, no matter how panic-stricken were the survivors, they'd rapidly recover and regroup into a mob-sized band howling vengeance.

The horses were safe enough and nickered as the men scrambled down the slope to them. Vaulting onto the saddle, the trio raked spurs and pulled carbines from scabbards, dashing down through the foothills toward the plain. Behind them the Sioux were already on the hunt, filling the night with their blood-lusting cries. Nickles wouldn't be taking this defeat lying down either, Fargo reckoned, but would surely try to turn it to his advantage. And, Fargo bet, the war party was riled enough to throw in with him, rifles or no rifles.

When they reached Lodgepole Creek and were again riding in the shelter along its waterline, they eased their horses to a trot. Once, Fargo glanced back and saw nothing of threat in the foothills. The second time he looked high over his shoulder, he spotted a dust cloud blurring the slopes.

"They're onto us," he said.

Brea smiled. "They won't catch up."

"Maybe not before we get to the train, *imbécile*, but then they will and . . ." Henri sighed, slitting his throat with his finger.

8

Pushing their exhausted mounts, Fargo and the two teamsters returned to the wagon train. Arriving, Fargo summoned Quinelle and the others to the corral and related what had occurred.

"We can expect an Indian attack anytime," he finished, "so everything better have been prepared. We won't get a second chance."

"All set, 'ceptin' the oil," Quinelle replied. "We'll pour it now, the way you tol' us to, out 'round on the bare ground."

Bridget Delahay heard the last part of Fargo's talk, and when the mule skinners had dispersed, she remarked, "Skye, I thought that Indians didn't attack at night."

"Tully Nickles is no respecter of time," he answered dryly.

"Nickles is leading their attack?"

"Using them. I think he's goading the Sioux to fight, instead of remaining behind to aid the wounded or, Indian-like, to mourn the dead."

Presently Tobac came with the news that a party on horseback was approaching. "But we're ready," he assured Fargo. "Oil'n all."

"Tell the men to light the fires when I shoot," Fargo ordered. Tobac sprinted away while Fargo made a quick round of the corral. Every man was in his place, either lying under the wagons or crouching behind walls of crates and barrels, watching tensely as distant specks gradually materialized out of the night.

"Maybe I can get through to the post at Crow River," Carajou suggested as the disorderly charge of Indians hurtled toward them.

Fargo hesitated. "I don't like to send a man out to die."

"We'll be dyin' either way. If I reach the army, there's a chance for all of us."

"Okay, Carajou," Fargo relented. "Pick your horse."

A few minutes later, Carajou rode by on a Chickasaw. "Hold 'em off, Capt'n."

Fargo nodded, watching as crates between a couple of the wagons were knocked down, and then Carajou leapt his mount through the gap and galloped off between the dark figures on the prairie. There were a half-dozen shots followed by Carajou's high-pitched yell. Fargo wasn't sure whether it was caused by pain or elation at getting through, but after that, he heard no more from Carajou.

The Sioux swerved in on them, yipping raucously, driving their painted ponies without stirrup or saddle, using only bitless rope bridles while throwing a cloud of arrows before them and lowering their lances for the kill. Fargo gauged their charge carefully. He waited as long as he could, then lifted his revolver and squeezed the trigger. The report echoed through the night. Immediately a number of small fires sprang up about thirty yards distant from the wagons.

"Fire at will," he called loudly.

Around him, rifles opened up at the now-illuminated figures of advancing Indians, while the mule skinners who ignited the fires raced back to the corral. With incredible speed, the fires leapt along the ground like great snakes, and in a moment they had joined to form a giant ring fueled by the oil poured on bare earth, where there was no danger of the flames spreading back to the wagons.

Up and down the line rifles were crackling, but there was no cadence to the firing as the skinners picked their shots. Fargo moved from man to man, encouraging, advising, firing along with them at the flitting figures beyond the wall of flame. Their withering gunfire caught the Indian charge in the van, piling up pony and rider. Yet still there were Sioux who came enraged, undaunted.

"Your oil's doin' it," Packard declared, chuckling. "We can see 'em, but they can't drive through." A pony swirled by and an arrow thwacked against canvas. Packard fired his carbine, reaching for his pistol. "If they do crowd in, Capt'n, I'll kill me a heap of 'em. Bridget? Gimme a fresh gun while you're there."

Bridget ducked under the wagon, taking his empty carbine and putting a loaded one close to hand. She was serene, fresh-faced despite the loss of sleep, seemingly unafraid as she made the rounds and loaded weapons as fast as she could.

Through a section where the fire was low, a bunch of riders suddenly appeared, heading toward the wagons. Gunfire was concentrated on them; three dropped at once and a fourth went tumbling when his mount fell over. The others wisely turned and fled back through the fire, trailed by the riderless ponies. That seemed to break the main Sioux charge, the war party veering off at angles, each brave fending for himself. Sighting carefully, the teamsters aimed their long guns and took a heavy toll of the fleeing Indians.

"That'll fix 'em," Jewett roared. "Come ag'in, yuh heathens."

"They will," Fargo assured him grimly. "Very soon, too."

Another man suddenly leapt through the flames. Holding up his hands, he sprinted forward yelling at the top of his voice. Staring at him, Fargo shouted, "It's Carajou. Don't fire!"

Shots from the Indian side of the fire, though, were whipping about the mule skinner. He dived over the barricade and sprawled on the ground inside the corral, flinching from the impact as his wounded right arm hit the earth.

"Muldoon! Get Upwind over here," Fargo called, eyeing the blood dribbling from Carajou's fingers. "Take it easy, Carajou. What happened?"

"I was chased," Carajou explained, gritting his teeth. "Damn hoss stepped in a prairie-dog hole and busted a foreleg. I crawled through the grass and got away, but was no use tryin' to hoof it to Crow River, so I figured I'd come back and try it again a-saddled."

Fargo shook his head. "You couldn't get through now," he said quietly. "They're all around us."

"I can make a try. God*damn* them gophers!"

"We'll need every man who can shoot. You'd best stay."

Grudgingly, Carajou went with Muldoon to have his wound treated. A lull in the shooting developed, and again Fargo toured the defenses. At one point he came upon Bridget, loading a Springfield carbine.

"You have a gun of your own?" he asked her. "A pistol?"

She took from one of the deep side pockets of her dress a relatively small, light, yet nonetheless lethal Colt Belt Model .36 pistol.

"Keep one bullet in it all the time," he warned.

"Nickles is a white man."

"Not out here, Bridget. If we're wiped out, it'll be blamed on the Sioux. Nickles won't want any survivors, and . . . Here they come!"

Once more the war party was down on them, screaming shrilly. Carbines were emptied, then revolvers were slamming shots into the onrushing mass of ponies and Sioux. The toll mounted, until a heaving crush of dead and wounded Indian and horseflesh filled the stretch where the fire burned low. The Regina teamsters never ceased reloading, firing, and reaching for more guns, their stolid defense behind the bulwark of wagons and cargo matching the fierce onslaught of more numerous but highlighted attackers. The battle ebbed and flowed for the balance of the night, the Sioux spending the final hours circling out of range, losing a few members, gaining nothing.

As the fire flickered out on the prairie, false dawn softened the sky. The teamsters crouched behind the barricade and peered into the semi-darkness, many of them wounded but so far only one dead, a taciturn mule skinner named Satsby. The Sioux' lack of firepower had held down the casualties, of course. Close to the wagons lay a score of Indian dead. The fact that they could spare five times that many didn't seem to mollify the survivors; out on the plain, the chieftains were having a heated conference with the red-headed Nickles.

"Them Injuns like to talk so much," Brea remarked, "let 'em talk all mornin' long."

Instead, Nickles and the chieftains began to rally the disorganized war party for another run. They were coming, Nickles' gunmen mixed in with the Sioux as they galloped toward the wagons, intending to ride right over the boxes and kegs stacked in between. Once they were inside the corral, the rest would be easy.

"Bolster the opening between one and seventeen," Fargo called, for the space between the first and last wagon was larger than the others, and a natural target for the Indians. Whatever else he might have ordered was lost in the thunder of guns as the Sioux closed within range, amid the throaty blasts of muzzle-loading rifles; the sharper cracks of repeaters; the pounding hooves and hair-raising cries as the Sioux poured at the wagons; the humming swish of their many arrows, the staccato reports of their few old Spencers . . . It was a deafening, roiling storm, all but ignored as targets were tracked and death was meted out.

Pressing his cheek against the stock of his Sharps, Fargo triggered off a shot and knocked the horse out from under a brave. He rolled and scrambled into a run, only to be downed when Velázquez' round struck him in the chest. Another brave swerved to pick up the wounded man. His head was blown apart by a slug from Quinelle.

By then Fargo had chambered and was ready to fire again, shoulder aching from his weapon's brutal recoil. He caught the brave nearest Tully Nickles, when Nickles veered aside at the last possible instant. The brave toppled against Nickles' horse, the horse shying and almost unseating the redhead, who hurriedly slewed the horse about, out of Fargo's gunsights.

The anxious war party rode to within twenty yards of the wagons before the deadly barrage from the teamsters halted them. Dozens were strewn on the ground, screaming among their kicking animals, while the galloping torrent surged by and reined up just out of range. There they milled restively, squabbling excitedly.

A couple of mortally wounded braves lay among the sprinkling of bodies. They stirred feebly, but never uttered a sound. A horse whinnied pitifully, its spine shattered. Brea and Henri the Canuck targeted them, three shots mercifully ending their agonies.

The shots also ended the Indians' debate. They spread out in a haphazard semicircle, sometimes slinging arrows, other times firing their carbines, their sniping scarcely a threat. Occasionally they'd try to sneak closer for a lucky shot, only to be spotted and driven back. The scattered harassment lasted for most of the morning, before Nickles and two of the younger chieftains could convince everyone else to line up for another drive.

"Try to down those two chieftains," Fargo advised as he once again darted from wagon to wagon. "If we can drop them and Nickles, the other chieftains might prevail and get the braves to pack it in."

Again the plain resounded with crackling gunfire, bloodcurdling screams, and the pounding hooves of the horses. The attackers headed toward the barricaded gap between the first and the last wagon, a flying wedge aimed straight at the most vulnerable part of the train's defenses.

Fargo emptied both rifle and revolver into the mob, blowing down five. He was reloading when they started to break through, their horses kicking at the crates and casks. Regina teamsters were grouping at the breach, firing at the Sioux, dragging them from their horses. Fargo saw Quinelle pick up one man bodily and heave him through the air; he also saw Nickles way in the back, urging his red brethren to push on harder, and he flashed a shot at him, but missed.

Tobac leapt over the barricade, a long "Arkansas toothpick" in his hand. The knife glinted in the morning sun as Tobac landed on the back of a Chadwick gunman, and his right arm rose and fell twice. There was blood on the thin blade when Tobac came back. The gunman lay spread-eagled flat, the ground beneath him becoming a thirsty crimson muck.

"Dammit, aim for the young chieftains," Fargo called, concentrating on one he had glimpsed in the melee. He hit the chieftain in the breastbone, rolled aside to avoid a tomahawk through his skull, and scanned for a glimpse of the other chieftain. That's all Fargo got, a glimpse, before bullets riddled the second young leader and his horse, and they both plummeted in a wild somersault, the chieftain actually bouncing when he landed.

It was too much for the morale of the Sioux warriors. Already stymied at the breach, they wavered and then broke. A grisly number remained squirming on the ground. Riderless horses tore away from the deadly encounter, squealing with fear and pain, while the surviving braves retreated, howling and confused—though some, including the older chieftains, were yelling and gesturing angrily toward Nickles and his gun crew, who were already tearing off.

"They're runnin'," Welch bellowed. "Send 'em to hell!"

As the teamsters unleashed volleys of gunfire, the departing Sioux melded into a single swirling mob, then sped furiously after the gunmen across the prairie. Shooting ceased when they passed out of rifle range, the mule skinners crawling from under wagons and behind stacked cargo, wiping the sweat from their grinning faces.

"Looks like they're ragin' at the gents who bumsteered 'em into this mess," Packard remarked, calmly wiping his knife on the bandages around his wounded thigh. "If they ain't, they should."

"Couldn't happen to a nicer bunch," Henri said, chuckling.

Her face stained with gunpowder, Bridget was more anxious than amused. "Just so it doesn't happen to us for a while. It was too close."

Fargo nodded. Jewett had died during the last charge, bringing casualties to two killed and ten down with slight to crippling injuries, and Fargo doubted they could've withstood another concerted assault. "Yeah, we'd better get organized and move out soon as possible."

"But the war party may be back," she protested. "We'd leave a trail an idiot could follow, and we'd be caught in line and slaughtered."

"There's that chance. We're a day from the Crow—a long, hard day that'll likely go some into night, and at any time the Sioux might track and strike us. But staying here gives us no chance at all."

"Nonsense! We've got weapons, food, plenty of water."

"Believe me, our supplies would mean nothing in the long haul. While we're holed up here, they'd be holed up out there, patiently waiting for us to run bare and make a break. They'd get us, Bridget."

That squelched any further argument. Everyone pitched in, working as best they could, some reloading weapons, the more able-bodied reloading cargo into wagons. A few of the corraled animals were dead, a few had to be put out of their misery, and the rest were watered and grained. Graves were dug and a brief ceremony was held for Jewett and Satsby. The fallen Sioux were left unburied, since the war party would return to collect them; yet the bodies were laid out respectfully for as Muldoon said, "It was senseless, but they were brave." The handful of gunmen remained untouched, unhonored, for as Carajou said, "The vultures can take 'em like they is—if the vultures will have 'em."

This difference in treatment wouldn't be lost

on the Indians, Fargo reckoned, and might earn enough respect to hold them back. Something had to stave them off. If not, if they hit, they'd smash a limping ruin of a train. It was not only under-teamed now but undermanned, what with two mule skinners dead and four so wounded they couldn't drive. Wranglers from Velázquez' crew replaced some; Fargo decided to pilot the head wagon; and two other wagons were hitched together with their shortened teams combined so the pair would move.

"Mount up," Fargo finally ordered, climbing onto the wagon seat alongside Bridget. "Wherever we find ourselves, come tomorrow morning, it's going to be a long ride ahead."

They veered southwest now, roughly in line with the army outpost's location on the Crow River. This headed them toward the far southern end of the Laramie Mountain range, though at such a slight angle, that they continued on the prairie throughout the day. Even when the sun became a slowly descending ball in the west, it was often masked by the tiers of foothills rising ahead and to their right.

With twilight, however, they approached the broken edges of the hills. Dusk fell softly, quietly, as they began threading a seemingly endless succession of bluffs and gulches; yet there were other stretches, as they broke out into a plateau or ledge, where the final sunset gleam would illuminate an expanse of terrain, a dazzling panorama of mountain and plain. Soon all grew shadowed, a breezy chill rustling draft-gnarled scrub and stirring eddies of grit over the invisible landscape.

The outfit slowed to a crawl as Fargo allowed

the lead team to set the pace across devious, vague flats and through obscured thickets and clumps of tall saltbush. Routinely they stopped for short rests, which now were the only times he could scout around. They'd thrown the Sioux off the hunt, perhaps, but until they reached the outpost, they could expect that anytime, anywhere, they were open to a raid.

Along about nine-thirty that night, Fargo reluctantly called another halt. He'd hoped to come upon an area where the wagons could be circled, but hadn't passed any place that wide for miles, and the view ahead didn't appear any more promising. The mules, though, were done in. So, out of necessity, he picked the next safest arrangement, parking in a natural depression bordered by rocks. Nothing appeared wrong on either side, nor did he notice anything peculiar when he checked up front and back behind. Nonetheless, he didn't like it.

While Fargo was away riding the circuit, the crew silently ate cold jerky and biscuits, the surrounding darkness an almost welcome shroud, masking their moody faces. Bridget tried to catch some sleep in the wagon, falling into a restless doze, only to be awakened by horseshoes striking bare stone. Her initial thought was that it was Fargo returning, but after a moment, when there were no other sounds or familiar voices, she sat up, fully awake.

"Skye?"

No response.

Puzzled, Bridget glanced out the front flap. "Skye?"

A mule brayed, chafing its leather collar.

Alarmed now, Bridget started to crawl out, pausing awkwardly on the wagon seat and sighing when she saw Fargo approaching on his Ovaro. She watched while Fargo dismounted and tied his horse to the tailgate, then she asked as he strode forward, "Why didn't you answer?"

"To what?"

"Me! I heard you and kept calling and—"

"You heard me?" Fargo cut in sharply. He stared for an instant, thinking, then raised his revolver and fired. "Stir awake, you knotheads, we've got visitors about," he shouted over the blast. Then his yell was swallowed in an explosion of shrill banshee yells.

Fargo leapt to the wheel hub, up to the seat, just as the screeching Indians burst into the narrow clearing. He hooked an arm around Bridget's waist and swept her with him through the flap, down flat to the wagon bed in a tangled, intimate embrace.

Bullets splintered the perch on which Bridget had been kneeling. The piercing yells, blasting carbines, and whirring arrows rose in a spiraling crescendo along the line of wagons, augmented by the cannonade from the teamsters' array of weapons, and increasingly accented by the squawls of the braves they were hitting. A mule brayed, dying, thrashing in its harness; and the high whinny from a wounded horse caused Fargo to wonder if his prized Ovaro had been mortally struck.

His Sharps was still tucked in that horse's saddle scabbard, but he had no intention of going outside to fetch it. He tugged out his revolver while Bridget stayed flat, knocked breathless, and all about them a whining, ricocheting hail of arrows and bullets punctured the sideboards and sieved the canvas cover. He was cocking the hammer when an ax blade slashed the canvas within inches of where Bridget lay. He dived back to her as the ax slashed again, and he fired through the rip. There was a choking groan, and the ax disappeared.

Swiftly Fargo darted for the rear flap, fearing that the Sioux would try boarding the tailgate. He pushed aside the flap, unwilling to make more of a target of himself than was necessary. But the area in back—in fact, the entire line of wagons stretching behind—was empty of Indians. He realized then that the gunfire and shouts were all coming from the teamsters, and that the raiders had withdrawn as suddenly as they'd attacked.

"What in hell?" he snapped loudly. "Who's still alive?"

By the answering chorus of roars, he deduced the entire crew had survived. Quinelle yelled, "A passel of Injuns sure ain't!"

"Pity," Fargo murmured, climbing down off the tailgate.

His and Bridget's horses were white-eyed and prancing, straining at their lines now tied to the wagon's rear bracing. Fargo spent a moment calming them, finding only minor scratches, then headed back along the train to check on the damage. He paused to confer with Upwind Muldoon, who was trying to plug a leak in a water barrel roped to the sideboard of one wagon. "Are any of the injured worsening?" he asked.

Muldoon shook his head. "Nobody's turned peaked yet."

Farther back, Carajou was dragging a dead mule away in spite of his wounded arm. Another dead mule hung slackly in its swing-team harness, pincushioned with arrows. Fargo went over and began unstrapping it from its singletree. "We're lucky to have any mules still left alive," he said. "We fared better than we had a right to, especially considering I was supposed to spot them and didn't."

"Hell, boss, this section's riddled with darker an' tinier hidey-holes than a wench's muff in a coal mine. That you could give any warnin' a'tall is plumb remarkable. 'Sides, it was a crazy raid. I don't know who was more surprised—us, or the Injuns when they didn't catch us nappin'? They came in fast, p'raps ten or so on each side, got lambasted for their effort, and just kept on a-scootin' faster'n ever." Carajou gazed around at the litter of dead raiders and their mounts, then trudged back to unchain the swing-team doubletree. "Dammit, though, my Chickasaw bolted berserk and broke his hock. I don't want to do what has to be done."

Gently Fargo offered, "If it'll help, I'll do it."

"Thanks, boss, no. I helloed him as a colt, so it's up to me to say good-bye." Carajou sighed and added with a twinge of disgust, "Now, your dopey nag just stood nonchalant, like it was in the middle of a daisy field, and didn't get as much as a hair mussed."

"Odd. Indians usually run off available stock," Fargo remarked, stepping across to one of the dark-skinned figures. Mortally shot, the man twitched a little, grimacing a hideously painted face in black, red, and white stripes. Hunkering,

Fargo ran fingers through the man's light brown hair, and he wet a fingertip and rubbed a spot on the bony jawline. The brownish-red color lightened and showed dingy white skin and beard stubble where he rubbed.

"Thought so," Fargo said. "You work for Chadwick, don't you?"

The gunman stared with pain-flecked eyes. He stopped struggling for breath, as if in the haze of death he were trying to collect himself, to think.

"Sure, you're one of Nickles' boys. You all must've lost the war party, then circled back and stripped the dead Indians, figuring if any of us chanced to survive your butchering sneak attack, we'd blame it on the Sioux. That's how it was, wasn't it? *Wasn't it?*"

The gunman sucked a convulsive, bubbling breath. His fists clenched, his lips stirred feebly, frothing red. "Ah . . . ah . . ." he sighed, the cords in his brown throat tightening. "Ah . . . Fuck you."

And he died.

Fargo straightened, frowning, and returned to Carajou. "Did you catch a good look at any of the ones who got shot?"

"Hell's fire! When I'm killin' Injuns, I ain't got time to look."

"Go look now. In fact, we'll all go see if we can find any who might live long enough to reach the outpost and talk," Fargo added, leaving Carajou scratching his hair, perplexed.

Puzzlement quickly gave way to startled outrage and lurid invective. "Renegades! An' I took 'em as Sioux! Traitorin' crap! The sonsabitches are scummier'n any red devil." The mule skinners raved profanely while prowling among the bodies, but the few they discovered still alive were quickly diagnosed by Muldoon as being dead without knowing it.

Fargo was left in a bitter mood. They needed only one gunman capable of confessing to collar Nickles and, possibly, to smoke out Chadwick. Instead, they just had anonymous corpses unable to support their story, prove their claims of when and where who did what to whom.

"Good try," he told them, trying to hide his disappointment. "We better get on our way again. There's a chunk of rolling yet to do, and no telling what'll be down around our ears if we tarry."

9

Shortly before eleven, they climbed a hilly spur flanking the Crow. Turning westward and following the river, they remained on alert against further attack while watching for any one of the undoubtedly numerous trails leading to the army post. Pretty soon they came across a faint wagon path, and following its meander through stands of timber and pockets of hardy brush, they eventually reached the wide bowl of the upland valley containing the settlement.

Occasionally in the past, Fargo had heard the place referred to as Russell's, presumably after the fur trader who either founded it or sold it, though nobody seemed quite certain. As far as he knew, it had no name, not officially, and probably wouldn't until a fort was established or the railroad came through. But to call it anything, even a settlement, was a kindness. It was a motley hodgepodge of dingy, patched tents, clapboard shanties, and sod hovels that looked like the ground had merely swollen into shack-sized tumors, all dumped haphazardly among the boulders and woods of the shallow slopes and interconnected by rubbish-strewn footpaths.

Central, of course, was the old fur trade post. Now serving as the hub of a small, isolated military garrison, it was surrounded by a stout palisade that couldn't have been over a hundred yards long on each wall. The two largest civilian structures lined the road near the palisade gates: a goodly sized wooden building with the painted legend EMPORIUM, SUPPLIES & SUNDRIES across its facade; and the SILVER SLIPPER saloon, built of planks and *terrones*, bricks spaded from the earth rather than molded and dried, and with a big buffalo hide draped across its entrance like a front door.

Lanterns were aglow within the palisade, indicating activity despite the midnight hour. Outside, the Emporium was shuttered closed, but there was lamplight fanning from the saloon's windows and doorway, which was cluttered with patrons. As the wagon train approached, Fargo could see that many of the fresh-air idlers were off-duty troopers. Mingling with the uniforms were plenty of bearded, leather-skinned prospectors and settlers, or surly, hard-featured jiggers heavy on the gun and light on the law.

"It's not black enough," Bridget murmured.

Fargo knew what she meant: darkness was blurring rather than concealing the scabrous encampment around the post; still, he thought, at least the night was dulling it to a uniform squalor more mediocre than menacing. Or so he imagined, until the train drew close enough to the saloon for him to discern individuals among the pack in front.

He stared, growling, "Well, I'll be damned."

"No doubt, Skye. What of it?"

"Look at that bunch, about midway. Y'see Nickles? And in beside him, there's Luther Chadwick wearing a gray cutaway sack suit."

"You're right. I can understand Nickles here, but Chadwick?"

"He sure didn't come early to greet us. Likely he wanted to be on hand to mourn us when we failed to show up, then to bury Regina by wangling a new contract on the spot." Fargo grinned sardonically. "Kind of premature of Chadwick, but, hell, now he can cheer our arrival. Hey, and take a gander at Nickles' southpaw," he added, indicating the redhead's left arm in a sling. "I wonder how he got hurt, eh?"

Bridget matched his smile, but remained silent.

Moments later, when the wagons began pulling abreast of the saloon crowd, Fargo nodded at Chadwick, mockingly doffing his hat.

"That's right, show us you still got your hair on," Chadwick gibed, moving around in front of a hitch rack. "Otherwise we'd figure to find your locks hanging from some brave's scalp belt."

Snickers rippled through the crowd, and one pug-ugly loped out into the roadway, poking at a flea-bitten mule. "Look, it's alive," he hooted. The laughter grew loud and derisive with taunts.

Fargo sensed something deliberate in this gathering. It prompted him to make sure that his jacket was tucked away from the butt of his Colt and that his Sharps was still where he'd moved it from his saddle, propped by the seat within handy reach. And while eyeing the scornful group, he stifled his anger, keeping his expression affable as he focused on Nickles and asked, "Hey, Tully, have an accident?"

Nickles lost his laugh, his lips tightening, then twisting in a forced grin. "Yeah, m' damn gun popped off when I was cleanin' it."

"Hope it doesn't fester and rot on you," Fargo said, smiling, and regarded Chadwick again. "Since you're worried about my hair, Luther, I guess you must've heard of our running scrap with the Sioux, eh?"

Chadwick nodded, eyes narrowing.

"Word sure travels spritely hereabouts," Fargo marveled, then leaned forward as if to confide. "Here's some news that might not have gotten through to you yet, Luther. To hell with race, blood, color, we've been killing any sort who interferes with this outfit. Lots of them."

"If you say so, but why tell me?" Chadwick snapped.

"Oh, thought you might care to know," Fargo replied casually, "to save misunderstandings in case some of your boys come to visit."

Chadwick's face paled, then flushed red. "That's nigh to insinuatin', and not a man in this territory is fool enough to accuse me of backing such a play. You better not be the exception."

"Seems we're the exception just bucking you, but then, you've never showed so much in the open before. Careless of you, Luther, to rely on a notorious numbnuts like Nickles. Or were you strapped?" With that, Fargo's wagon rolled on ahead, leaving Chadwick sputtering, the veins in his neck throbbing visibly above his white collar.

For a moment Tully Nickles raged worse than his boss, snapping and gnashing like a rabid hound frothing on a leash. "Oh, yeah? Oh, yeah? I used m' smarts to—" Squelched abruptly by a livid snarl from Chadwick, Nickles blurted a low, "Oh, yeah," as if recalling orders, then pointed at Henri the Canuck, whose wagon was now heading abreast of the saloon, and raucously laughed while he jeered, "Wal, if it ain't ol' Hoocher Henri, the Upchuck Canuck hisself. Thinks he's a skinner an' can drive them crow-bait carcasses he calls mules. C'mon, Henri, fall off your seat here for a real short crawl."

Henri didn't bother to stop his wagon. He sprang from the box seat and landed with legs akimbo, bent at the knees, whip swirling. "No Consolidated *âne puant*—stinking jackass—can talk that way without tasting my leather, Tully Nickles."

And his braided lash was unfurling behind him. Nickles tried to dodge aside, clawing for his revolver. But Henri's forearm reversed and his snake ripped forward, cracking like a shot as it slit Nickles' right ear, temple, and cheek. Nickles howled, stumbling backward, forgetting about any draw and slapping his gunhand against the bleeding welt across the side of his face.

Already Regina teamsters were jumping from their wagons. And as though their rash fury was what the hard cases in the crowd had been waiting for, there came a sudden eddying move as these guys began to shove past the other spectators and, bristling with weapons, surged out along the roadway. But they had waited a second too long.

The moment Fargo had glanced back and caught the conniving byplay between Chadwick and Nickles, he'd realized why so many *hombres* swelled the crowd, realized they had gathered here by no mere chance. So when Henri had dropped off his wagon, Fargo immediately grabbed his Sharps and leapt down running. Before the gun thugs started their push, even before Nickles hit full bellow, Fargo reached Henri as he was stretching to flail again. Fargo clubbed Henri in the solar plexus with his rifle butt, knocking Henri flat with a startled, breathless curse.

Deafening that curse was the thunderous rifle shot Fargo cannoned low above the heads of the crowd. Its shattering blast instantly struck a stunned hush. Gun thugs in the process of drawing their pistols paused abruptly and eased off instead. Chadwick also hesitated, left hand opening his jacket, right hand reaching across to a shoulder holster, calloused fingers grazing a double-action .44 Starr. All his crew, just launching their rush against the teamsters, halted like a band of snubbed horses. Some had one boot on the porch and one on the ground—among these was the brown-haired man who'd helped Nickles dicker with the Sioux chieftains; now his face, with its scarred upper lip, was turned to Fargo, blank from shock. The only one moving was Nickles, understandably, diving into the saloon for aid. And the only one with a weapon unleathered was Fargo, standing grim and angry, smoking Sharps and cocked Colt commanding the whole scene. He spoke to Henri from the side of his mouth, eyes scanning the others.

"Get back to your wagon, Henri. I told you in Fort Laramie and will not again: keep rolling no matter how much they goad you, and stop taking up fights that can't help us, only maim us."

Henri struggled to his feet and hunched for a moment, gulping in air, his chest heaving. His chiseled Canuck features looked dour and hostile as a blizzard in his home province, and Fargo could tell that a storm was brewing in Henri. But Fargo's own craggy face had a harsh, granite appearance just then, and Henri knew Fargo well enough to have seen that countenance before, and to know what it meant. With a muttered curse, Henri picked up his whip, then climbed up onto his wagon seat.

Fargo ordered the rest of his crew back in that same hard, flat voice. Chadwick's bunch began to shift, and Fargo paused as he stalked up to the lead wagon, surveying them with dark mistrust.

"Anybody wants a slug through his brisket, just make another wrong move," he warned loudly, mounting the wagon-box seat and gathering the reins. "All right, Regina, str-i-i-ng out!"

This last was one helluva shout, which Fargo gave as the lead wagon lurched into movement, jerking as each span of mules leaned forward against the hames. He grinned at Bridget, who appeared shaken and distraught. Then he craned to glance back, meeting Chadwick's apoplectic glare with a sardonic smile.

As the string neared the palisade gates, a trooper walking the rampart with a rifle on his shoulder saw them and stood ready. The sergeant of the guard was called, and after a cursory inspection, he ordered the gates swung open. Whipping and cussing, they rolled in.

Around the palisade's inner perimeter were the militia buildings and a sutler's store. The sutler's was a dinky hut that, Fargo surmised, was merely a branch of the Emporium outside. The militia consisted of recently constructed troop billets, warehouse, farrier's shed, and stable barn, plus a large old cabin that had been converted from the fur trade post to the regimental headquarters.

Lugged by rackabone teams, seventeen wizened Conestoga freighters crossed the parade and halted before the headquarters. The heady scent of success hung on the air, and smelling it made Fargo beam as he climbed down, helping Bridget. By rights the teamsters should've been dead-tired, but they milled about, garrulously eager, mirroring Fargo's fervid smile, that grin of savage-wrested victory.

"You look obnoxiously smug," Bridget told them, though she too was smiling with relief and pride. "Don't forget, we're not finished till Colonel Garabedian signs his acceptance and awards our contract."

"Well, let's see if the colonel's awake."

"He wouldn't be now, and if he were, he wouldn't see us," Bridget argued, following Fargo into headquarters. "We'll make an appointment, Skye. The army's strictly formal about obeying rules and regulations."

Fargo just looked at her. He'd dealt with a number of remote garrisons such as this, overlooked, ignored, then forgotten. When an outpost was left on its own, he knew, it developed a mind of its own.

The orderly on night duty had no mind of his or anyone else's. He refused to do anything for them, from disturbing the colonel to making an appointment to arranging care for the badly wounded teamsters. They were at an impasse, which Fargo seriously contemplated breaking by breaking the orderly's neck, when a bear of a man entered through a rear door. He had dark eyes and whiskers that bristled, thick and unruly, and wore a rumpled field "undress" uniform with the eagles of a colonel. So Fargo immediately introduced Bridget and himself.

"Spank me afire, Regina finally showed," Colonel Garabedian declared heartily. "I've been opinin' you poor souls had all croaked by now." He gave Fargo an appraising glance as he ushered them into his office. "Not you. You look too bone-marrow deep mean to kill."

Chairs, a table near the window, a flat desk, and a brass spittoon were the furnishings. Sitting, Fargo watched Garabedian settle at his desk as if muscle and bone were weary, his eyes having a heavy-lidded gaze, and his breath . . . Fargo had already chanced to whiff that: the colonel was swacked. No, he was half-swacked, past tipsy but not stinko, from having nipped all evening for lack of anything better to do. Garabedian had literally been bored stiff.

Bridget shot Fargo a glance of anxiety and exasperation, indicating she knew Garabedian was potted, after she laid her wad of order copies, manifests, and freight bills on his desk. "Except for six barrels of oil, we've hauled all the army goods listed here, and are just waiting to unload," she told Garabedian, having the sense to swallow her disapproval and to act as if nothing was amiss.

"We'll start things going, Miz Delahay, but we can't wrap up everything tonight," Garabedian cautioned, regarding the papers with no vast enthusiasm. Then, as he began leaning to open a bottom desk drawer, he asked, "Tell me, how'd you manage to lose the oil?"

Fargo explained briefly. Listening, Garabedian brought up a tin cup and a quart jug, poured a drink, and when Fargo was done, he told Bridget, "I'm off-duty tonight. I trust I'm not offending you?" When Bridget courteously shook her head no, Garabedian tossed back the drink and asked Fargo, "What route did you take?"

"Straight down Goshen Hole, due south through the plains east of the Laramies to Lodgepole Creek, and directly cut for here."

"Why that way?" Garabedian asked, pouring another drink.

"Quickest."

Garabedian chortled at Fargo's laconic answer. "Here, have a suck," he offered, sliding the jug across to Fargo. "Aside from that time you used the oil, did you run into other trouble on your trail?"

"Yeah." The jug held raw corn whiskey the fumes alone could have etched crystal, and made Fargo's eyes water. "Plenty."

"Sioux?"

"They'll recall us."

"Any others?"

Fargo shrugged noncommittally and sampled a swallow. A liquid torch seared down his throat, igniting a black-powder charge in his stomach that left him gasping, shivering compulsively. He got up and placed the jug gingerly back on the desk. "What'n hell's in it?"

Rising, Garabedian hooked the jug handle with his finger. "I'm given to understand by the moonshiner," he replied, standing with the jug, grinning across at Fargo, "that there's a chaw of tobacco in for blend, and red-pepper squeezings for spice." He swigged heftily straight from the jug this time and began to grow apple-cheeked but mischievous. "Mist' Fargo, I dare wager I could whump you."

Bridget gasped, appalled. "No!"

But there was no time for her to protest. And this was no time for Fargo to relax. Garabedian tore across the desk, chuckling, lunging, to surprise Fargo off guard, hands reaching as though to throttle him. Fargo caught him by the wrists and yanked him farther across. Garabedian planted his feet, legs levering, chortling as he wrestled himself and Fargo toward his side. Obviously he was in a wringy mood to scrap from that popskull booze, or from dead-post boredom—Fargo didn't know and didn't care.

Besides, Garabedian had stopped his laughing. Fargo had him by the beard now, and pivoting, he braced his back against the side of the desk and hauled Garabedian over his shoulders. Both men hit the floor with stunning impact, but Fargo was on top, fists snagging in Garabedian's whiskers. Already the orderly had barged in the door, let loose a bleat, and scurried back out; now the doorway was jammed with troopers, who evidently were used to their colonel brawling in his office, for they watched without interfering while Fargo banged Garabedian's head on the floor a few times, then got up grinning.

Rising to his hands and knees, Garabedian felt his cheeks tenderly. "Clear out! Shut the door," he barked, and the door slammed closed. He got to his feet then, smiling genially at a quite aghast Bridget. "Your captain's a ring-tailed wampus, Miz Delahay," he said, and went to his desk, righted his chair, and sat down. "Let's get back to the varnish, what say?" He shoved the jug toward Fargo.

Fargo shook his head. "After our business is done."

Garabedian winked at Bridget, further disconcerting her. "This catamount is smarter'n he looks." He pushed aside the jug and picked up the sheaf of papers. "All right, a few minutes, please." He perused quietly. "No gross errors sprang out," he said when he was finished. "Congratulations. I didn't expect you yet, y'know, not before the deadline, if, frankly, at all." He chuckled. "Nor did Consolidated. Sorry to mention 'em, but I'm tickled by your deflating Mr. Chadwick and his crew, who've been windily insisting Regina's jinxed, you'll default, and your train would wreck from one disaster to another."

"Not for lack of trying," Bridget murmured cryptically.

"Yeah, life is hard. You gotta be harder," Garabedian replied, misunderstanding. "You gotta give Chadwick his due, he's rougher than fate. He's a length from being old-maid respectable, sure, but I've never heard of any skunks roped to his coattails, either."

Bridget glanced at Fargo. "I think the colonel

should know." Fargo merely shrugged, so she eyed Garabedian and concisely related the events involving Chadwick's forces, first raid to last.

"Gun-running! Bossing outlaws who pose as Indians!" Garabedian sat up, sobering, concerned yet skeptical. "Unbelievable! Even if I did, I can't have Chadwick arrested on unsubstantiated charges."

"And we don't have a shred of evidence," Fargo admitted, shaking his head. "If we'd caught any gunman alive tonight, chances are they'd have jawed to save their necks, but no such luck. And we need to rope them or Nickles red-handed for us to lasso Chadwick."

"Don't even count on that," Garabedian advised. "Chadwick's richer'n sin, and as powerful, with plenty of influence. If he denied your accusations—and I can't imagine he'd admit to them—he could throw considerable weight, probably bloody your reputations before it was over. Desperate rival resorting to slander, y'see my drift?"

Bridget nodded. "I also see Skye may've been right to stay mum till we had something solid. Forget we mentioned it, please."

"Consider it done." Garabedian leaned back, tenting fingers. "Other than your badly wounded, who'll bed in our infirmary, I'm afraid your caravan's got to camp outside the post. The quartermaster sheds open at O-six-hundred. Leave all this paperwork with me, that's what I've got clerks for, and assuming the supplies are in as good a shape, I'll give Regina a permanent contract. Now, is there anything else?"

There was nothing else, not until sunup.

Shortly the creaking wagons filed from the post in a welter of snapping whips and violent curses. The mule skinners were sour-tempered, the grinding strain of the trip having rawed their nerves, the rumpus at the saloon having stirred their contrary juices, and now this delay in delivery plunging a heartened spirit into a frustrated, rancorous, ugly mood. Henri the Canuck was the worst of all.

After some tedious searching, a suitable campsite was located about a mile from the settlement, along a bend of the Crow. A couple of acres wide, it was a fairly level patch of brambles and grasses suitable for grazing. An old river channel lay on their right, curving like a drawn bow with an undercut wall of boulders behind it, while on their left stretched a bar of coarse gravel dotted by large rocks and hardwood saplings. Otherwise the riverbank and surrounding sides were overgrown with entangling brush and thickets of aspen, pine, and cottonwood.

Sullenly muttering, the teamsters corralled the train. Lanterns were set out, and by their feeble glow, the animals were tended and a final check made of the camp. Bedrolls began to be laid out.

"I ain't sacking," Henri then declared belligerently. "I feel a thirst comin' upon me, like for a nightcap maybe at that saloon."

"That'll do, Henri," Fargo said flatly. "Nobody's leaving."

For a moment Henri stood there, hairy hands opening and closing spasmodically. Some of the teamsters started gathering, adding their surly support. "We're going," Henri growled, and shook out a coil of his whip. "We ain't seen a drap of liquor 'twixt Fort Laramie an' here, but you can't keep us no longer from having a drink. Or from exchangin' howdies with some fellers we might bump into at the bar."

"I guess it wasn't clear enough for you before. The saloon is packed with strong-arm gunnies hired to do what they did already: get you angry. When you're fighting-blind mad, they'll coldly, deliberately bust every bone in your body, including your solid stone head."

"Not if we hit first, and hit hard," Brea countered.

Henri, nodding, shook out another coil. "Step aside."

The men began clustering in, voices raising. There wasn't much difference between them and a herd of mules just before a stampede, and everything hinged on the rummy Canuck now.

Realizing this, Fargo settled himself, muscles tight across his belly, and spoke in his flat, adamant voice again. "The only thing you'll hit first and hard is the bottle. While they're fighting you, you'll be fighting rotgut booze—and'll lose."

The full length of Henri's whip lay on the ground, and his forearm rippled as he tensed his grip. "Get out of the way, or else!"

"Don't be dumb," Fargo retorted. "Get drunk, disabled, tossed in the brig, and you can't unload tomorrow or defend the train from—"

Bellowing a mule skinner's gargantuan oath, Henri snapped his whip behind his head. The men about him surged forward, yelling, and Fargo knew whatever he said now didn't matter.

Henri had an incredible swift skill with his blacksnake, and though Fargo had seen it coming, his revolver barely cleared leather when that howling whip slashed across his wrist, knocking his Colt flying. He grunted with the sudden sharp pain, taking an instinctive pace backward. Then they were on him, a shouting, swearing bunch with Henri's savage, sneering face looming up out of the press.

The sheer weight of them forced Fargo to his knees. But he was a big man filled with a big rage, and he wasn't finished yet. As the closest, Velázquez, lurched hard into him, he drove upward, grabbing the hostler's thick torso and using his momentum to fling him on over his shoulder. With Velázquez still pitching through the air behind him, Fargo lunged forward, smashing Brea full in the chops. Brea staggered back, windmilling, tripping up Packard and a couple of others, who stumbled over his body and fell across him.

Even as Fargo struck Brea, he twisted sideways and caught Henri with his left arm. Then he rammed his shoulder into the Canuck and heaved him backward. Losing his balance, Henri fell among onrushing men, knocking one aside, crashing into another pair and halting them. Their forward surge stymied at that instant, Fargo took a swift step back so there was a little cleared space between him and Henri. Already Henri had struggled free of the tangle, and roaring furiously, he sailed his whip behind his head again.

And again a gunshot stopped him from flaying a second time. It was the sharp crack of a pistol, not the stunning thunderclap of Fargo's Sharps, yet it effectively stalled the melee. A blank look came to

Henri's face, then he brought his hand back down so he could see it. The bullet had cut the braided lash neatly from the whipstock, and all he held was that handle. The rest lay on the ground behind him.

Bridget Delahay stood from where she had shot, her Colt Belt Model .36 still smoking in her small hand. Her voice had a cool, unshaken sound. "You've just been aching to take a swipe at somebody, Henri, and we won't know peace till you do. But it's to be done fair."

The others shifted away from Henri, careful not to make any wrong moves, not against someone who'd shot with more skill than any gal should rightly possess. Bridget cast an anguished glance at Fargo, well aware that the only chance of saving Regina lay in his beating Henri.

Henri dropped his whipstock and rushed. Fargo moved forward, bending a little to meet the shock of Henri's charge. To a sudden scuffle of boots and the resulting puff of dust, the two men collided with a singular, giving, fleshy thud.

Henri had his knee up as he came. Fargo twisted and took it on his thigh, shoulder moving with the turn as he straight-armed a knuckler into Henri's face. Henri stumbled awry. Fargo closed, doubling him over with a jab under the heart, and was about to straighten him with an uppercut when Henri rammed in, butting. The air exploded from Fargo and he sank like a deflating balloon. Henri's calloused hands groped for his face, thumbs seeking his eyes. Fargo battled upward, jerking his head away from Henri's hands, driving out with a weak left into Henri's belly. Then a stronger right. And he stood erect again, pistoning his fists into the Canuck.

Henri absorbed the blows, grunting thickly to the first, then taking a step backward. He grunted to the second and stepped back. The third one knocked him over into the dirt, flat on his back.

Muttering curses, he slowly got up, shaking his head like the stubborn bull he was. Bridget watched them, her face pale and set. The teamsters spread out, shouting encouragement to Henri as they had to Fargo when he'd gone down, less interested in who won than in seeing both continue to smash each other to pulp. Obligingly Henri moved in. He ducked a right and pounced with his arms wide, taking Fargo's left punch so he could grapple.

What happened next was a little too fast for the crowd to follow. Fargo's long leg snaked behind Henri's knee, and down they went rolling, until he got a leg under him and threw Henri away. His head rocked as Henri's hook caught him across the ear. Then Fargo was striking out again, following Henri back relentlessly. He caught the man on the jawbone with a right. Henri reeled, almost falling. A left sank into his belly, drawing a wheeze. The right slammed him in the face again, and he sprawled again on the ground.

Fargo swayed there above the skinner, panting, blood dribbling from his cut lip. The crew yelled lustily with calls to get up. It took an eternity for Henri to rise on his elbow, another to sit up. He spat some teeth, some blood, then tried to stand. His struggle failed and he sank back to his elbow, staring guardedly at Fargo. Both knew the rules or the lack of them, knew that having rebelled and lost, Henri should be stomped, disabled or dead, by the boss. The others lapsed into silence, the whole sweating batch of them tensing for Fargo to claim his right.

Instead, Fargo extended his hand.

A pause, then Henri accepted it, grinning sheepishly as he was helped up. "Eh, I'm spoiling no more. You're right, I get crazy mad sometimes, but nobody can say I hold a grudge when it's over." He turned to the others. "An' maybe the capt'n clobbered some sense into me. If anyone tries sloping out, he'll now have two to stop him."

There was indecision in some of the men's faces, and not all of them would meet Henri's and Fargo's burning gazes.

"Tomorrow night you can sweep that bar to the floorboards with one another," Fargo promised. "But tonight I won't have any swill-belly mule skinner get suckered into a fight that's rigged, dammit, to cripple if not kill my entire crew. I won't give Luther Chadwick the one last chance he's got to destroy Regina. Now, turn in."

And that was that.

Or so they thought.

10

Fargo did not sleep in his bedroll that night.

He drowsed in the lead wagon. The flaps were pulled closed and freight was piled up all around, making darkness too deep for him to see Bridget. He could certainly feel her nude body pressing alongside him, and could certainly hear her—Bridget in a chatty mood, whispering innocuous questions and then murmuring on.

"I've had schooling, too. Got through my seventh reader, Skye, but from there I was on my own. Mom taught me accounting; so, after she passed away, I took over keeping the company books and things. Do you mind me talking?"

"No." It was true; Fargo knew she needed an outlet.

"Oh, I'm just prattling. I'll shut up."

Shifting, Fargo stroked her cheek affectionately to confirm that it was all right, but that only seemed to make her shut up. She kissed him instead, a lingering press of lips while his fingers wandered from her cheek to one breast, teasing her nipple erect. His hand glided down across her smooth belly to the soft, pulsing warmth below as she moaned, her flesh quickening to his caresses.

Now she spoke again, her voice sighing in his ear. "We shouldn't risk it a second time, Skye. Somebody could come."

"That, Bridget, is the whole idea." He kissed her, then the nape of her neck; the breast, with its engorged nipple, he suckled between his lips. Bridget responded fiercely, squirming against him, draping one bent leg over him in an effort to thrust closer, then hesitating, withdrawing her swollen breast.

"I want to taste you," she whispered, curling to return his kisses, moving the blanket that had been covering them so she could dart her tongue across his tiny nipples ... swirling lower along his taut abdomen ... then still lower, probing and exploring the fleshy shaft of his erection, finally plunging her mouth voraciously over it, swallowing him in a softly clinging pressure.

Fargo felt his hips writhing, stirring with sensations, a hungry vacuum drawing all his vital juices to his groin. And Bridget seemed to be enjoying this almost as much as he, clawing at his buttocks, her tongue licking and twining, her teeth gently nipping, her lips firmly stroking, impatiently greedy to savor the tumultuous eruption building in him.

"You better quit while you're ahead," Fargo panted.

Bridget laughed, low and liquid. He drew her straight up against him in a close embrace while her hips slackened, widening to cradle him.

"Now," she crooned breathlessly, devouring the whole of him up inside her small belly as she arched her back off the wagon bed. "Now . . ."

When impaled to the hilt, Bridget kicked her feet out and locked clawing arms and legs firmly around Fargo's tensely moving body. He felt her eager young muscles tightening smoothly around him in a pressured action of their own, and he set his mind to the delicious ecstasy of the moment. She wrapped her limbs tightly, sinking her fingernails into his back, rhythmically matching Fargo's building tempo while his pent-up orgasm hovered on the verge of erupting.

She pushed against him, squeezing harder as she sensed his imminent release. Shivering uncontrollably, she bit her arm to keep from crying aloud as Fargo spurted violently into her, then shuddered convulsively with the impact of her responding climax. Her awakened flesh undulated, then collapsed beneath him as she savored a contented satiation. Soon they dozed, remaining firmly embraced . . .

Shortly Fargo awoke again and lay listening to Bridget's heavy breathing. He hadn't been aroused by premonition, or by some warning note of impending doom, as he had with Delores in Fort Laramie. He simply had to take a leak. So carefully easing from Bridget, Fargo dressed quietly and slipped out through the front flap.

Clouds had been forming through the night, and in the moonless gloom of this early-morning hour he could see little. The enclosure was quite dark, and there was no sign of the nighthawks on guard outside the corral. He lowered the flap and quickly clambered over the chains fastening the wagon's front wheels to the rear wheels of the wagon ahead, then trotted to the edge of the field and played a dog's respects to a tree.

Returning, however, Fargo abruptly flattened against the wagon and stood stock-still. Directly across the circle, he caught the glimpse of a drifting shadow. He could see merely the silhouetted head and hat of a dark figure against the filthy white canvas of a wagon, but that was enough to make him wonder. Walking out in the darkness, he started on a swift circuit of the camp.

One of the nighthawks loomed up out of the grass, rifle barrel gleaming faintly. Fargo murmured, "It's okay, set put." The hawk grunted and disappeared.

Pausing ten yards from the wagon where he'd seen the man, Fargo slid out his revolver, then pushed through the grass stealthily until he reached the wheel of the wagon. From underneath the bed rose snores and honks of a dead-asleep mule skinner. From up in the bed came soft rustlings that might indicate a foraging mouse . . . or a rat.

Placing one boot on the wheel spoke, Fargo reached up and grabbed a guy rope with his left hand. Stepping onto the wide tire rim, he grasped another rope and moved to the slight opening between flaps. A match flared just then, and Fargo caught a brief glimpse of the man's face. It was the brown-haired, scar-lipped pal of Nickles. Something started to hiss and sputter. A black powder cartridge. The man was lighting its fuse.

Instantly Fargo vaulted through to the top of the load, landing on the man's back. There came a startled curse as Fargo, chopping with his gun barrel, felt the man go limp. The fuse was sputtering merrily. Frantically Fargo ground it out beneath his heel.

In that moment of anxiety, Fargo was solely intent on the fuse. Then he was aware of a looming figure—the man, who'd merely been stunned, had recovered and was diving in a scramble out the flap. As Fargo wheeled, the man triggered a panicky shot, its slug droning past his ear. He loosed off from the hip, snap-firing. The man squawked in agony and plunged tumbling off the wagon, with Fargo in pursuit. But the bullet had taken him in the middle, and he only got as far as the ground, where he lay groaning as nighthawks and skinners came racing up.

"Injuns?" one of the teamsters yelled.

"No," Fargo said. "It's all right." He moved to the man and kicked his pistol from his hand. The man twitched, then was still. Nobody else was, the shots having awakened the entire camp. Men were pouring toward the wagon, armed and raising a hullabaloo.

An early arrival was Welch, for he'd been the one asleep under the wagon. "Say, didn't we see this'n among the Chadwick jiggers?"

"Yeah, siding Nickles," Brea confirmed. Hunkering, he pawed in the man's pockets and brought out a cartridge and more fuse. "Well, well, now we know what dirty raw job he was sent here to do."

"Already has done," Fargo corrected dryly, showing the stick and fuse he'd snuffed out in the wagon. And with the rest of the crew and Bridget now gathering around, he recounted what had occurred.

A council of war began then as one of the mule skinners declared harshly, "Like the boss says, Chadwick's got his last chance tonight, an' he's restorted to blowin' us outta our sugans from pure desperation."

"Guess he fears a reg'lar open attack might draw the army," Quinelle said, frowning. "This sure tempts me to agree with Henri, and take the play away from 'em. Hit 'em hard, fast, and permanent."

Bridget shook her head. "That listens swell, Tiny, but Chadwick has too many gunmen. I have better men"—she smiled confidently at the group—"but not so many of them. What do you think, Skye?"

"I think we'd better get ready for an attack."

"What d'you mean?"

"Well, look, it doesn't make much sense for one gent to have sneaked in here just to blast a few wagons. Chadwick isn't so stupid to believe that would force Regina to cave in, right?"

Quinelle snapped his fingers. "No reason not to hit back."

"It is, if the blasts were to be a signal. Chadwick may well have his bunch not far from here, set to raid us as soon as they hear the explosions and wipe out the train in our confusion."

"Bet you're right," Upwind Muldoon said. "By the time any soldiers could get here, we wouldn't be here to do no complainin'."

"How horrid," Bridget gasped. "What'll we do, Skye?"

"What Tiny suggested, take the play away from

them. They figure on surprising us, but now we can surprise them. Ambush them. We can hand them a sweet surprise package, make no mistake."

Tobac asked, "What if the mistake is yours?"

"Okay, assume I'm wrong, and nobody's out there preparing to storm us. We rig our trap for nothing—but lose nothing but sleep."

"You convinced me, boss," Quinelle stated. "Me and some o' the boys will ride out and form a reception committee." He slapped his thigh. "Hell'n spitting devils, this is gonna be fun."

Soon nine riders were galloping from camp, and what they might have lacked in numbers, they made up for in toughness and resolve. Staying behind were Bridget and the other teamsters with instructions where to send word in case of a flanking sneak attack. They'd also wanted to go, but were better off remaining due to their injuries.

Fargo picked the ambush site about a quarter-mile back along the trail they'd wagoned in on. He and the mule skinners spread out along the sides of a short draw, affording them both height and cover. Five minutes later, someone at the wagons touched off the two sticks of black powder. Everyone was anticipating the blasts, yet the sticks detonated with such brilliant force, that all along the draw men jerked behind their shelter. Then, as the noise and fire echoed across the woodland, they settled down again to await developments.

Crouching, Fargo stared uptrail like a cat watching a mouse hole. It wasn't much of a trail, more like an animal path that man had trammeled wider to bare earth, because the path was the only route through the surrounding timber. There'd been no sign of gunmen close by the wagons, but Fargo doubted that Chadwick would plan his raid that way. It'd be too risky for a gang to weasel through the tangled foliage undetected, whereas one man could sneak in and out, his explosive sabotage sowing panic, wrecking loaded wagons, and signaling the gang. Speed, not stealth, would then be most important, and the raiders would strike the fastest way, along this trail.

That is, if Fargo was correct.

The answer was not long in coming.

All of a sudden, Fargo could tell something was approaching. At first it was like an angry rumble of storm winds blowing south toward the river, but quickly it swelled to a deep, rhythmic pounding. The ground-drumming roll quickly sharpened into the thunder of horses' hooves, the wrench of saddles, the sharp oaths of men.

With the teamsters, Fargo focused on the far sweep of the draw, just as the first push of riders careened around a bend and entered it. Behind them streamed a looming flow of big men on big horses, driving toward the camp at a headlong clip. Fargo searched their midst and spotted Tully Nickles, the only one with his head and half his face turbaned in gauze bandages. And yes, there was Luther Chadwick riding in the middle, looking smugly confident. It was evident that he had his share of brute courage and had taken personal command to ensure success. Chadwick must have reckoned—and rightly so—that the vastly outnumbered teamsters would be hard-pressed to defend their wagons, much less mount a counterattack.

Consequently Chadwick and crew rode with a

free rein, nothing in their manner indicating they suspected any ambush. The trail blurred under their horses as they came abreast of the teamsters, thirty strong and far from asleep, but not as awake as they should have been either.

In that instant, the air cracked from the ripping gunfire pouring in from both sides. The staccato volley emptied three saddles and sent the others flying for cover, each man for himself. Fanning out right and left, the Chadwick gunnies began answering with pistol and carbine, the steady exchange of bullets punctuated by shouts and curses, and with Chadwick yelling orders and countermands. The gunmen, stooping low, began charging toward the boulders where the teamsters were holed. One man somersaulted backward; two more vaulted his sprawling body, only to be downed in turn.

Yet the teamsters were in a desperate bind, Fargo realized. They had surprised the gang and accounted for eight or nine casualties without receiving a wound. But the odds were still greatly against them, and now that the gunmen had also reached cover, it would only be a matter of time before the nine of them were whittled to zero. Whether by that time the army could arrive was another matter. If Colonel Garabedian was at all typical, the post would be a nest of boiled owls by now, in no condition to mount a rescue.

"Hold 'em, boys," Quinelle roared. "Hold 'em!"

The gunmen were coming. Urged on by Chadwick, they were swarming up through the rocks and trees, turning the trail and the shouldering draw into an inferno of blazing gunfire. Twice the mule skinners held them and sent them recoiling down. Twice the gunmen managed to rally and surge higher, blasting at the thin line of grim defenders. The battle became a riot of pistols and knives and hand-to-hand struggles.

An attacker, his pistol shot out of his hand, rushed Fargo with a razor-sharp hunting knife. He got to within a foot, slashing his heavy blade. Then, abruptly, his face went blank; between his eyes there appeared a rounded hole, with bluish edges. Right, left, other raiders were struck as Fargo and two wounded teamsters near him fired with the coolness of marksmen at a turkey shoot. But despite the number of gunmen lying injured or dying, despite the teamsters fighting like demons, they could not stem the Chadwick tide rolling over them.

Constantly on the lookout for Chadwick or Nickles, Fargo had to retreat to the vantage of a large clump of brush—out of which, unnoticed, a gunman arose with revolver in hand. At that moment, Fargo glimpsed Chadwick and drew a bead with his rifle. Then a man dashed between them, and Fargo had to hold his fire. But the gunnie in the brush did not, and triggered. Quinelle swayed, clasping his arm, his own pistol dropping from nerveless fingers.

Too far to be of help, Fargo swore as he watched Quinelle fall and more gunmen sweep upward to engulf him and the nearby teamsters. Now other gunmen, including Chadwick, were remounting to spur their horses along the draw like a charge of cavalry. Only Fargo and two, maybe three, teamsters remained able enough to stand between the advancing horsemen and the wagon camp.

Hastily reloading, Fargo cradled the rifle stock

and fired one shot, then loosed a string of them as fast as he could chamber and trigger. Reports from the other two or three teamsters came in ragged salvos. The riders wavered, two going down and a third slumping.

But it was not enough.

"Fall back to the wagons," he shouted. "We'll fort there!"

The others, realizing they'd die for nothing if they stayed, and eager to warn those at the wagons so that a final stand could be made, joined Fargo in a scrambling dash for their horses. Then in a wild gallop, Fargo and the two—only two—teamsters raced along the trail toward the wagon camp, desperate to reach it before the bullets of the pursuing gang found them. Behind, the draw appeared choked with raiders, their revolvers and rifles blasting away in erratic though massive volleys at Fargo, Tobac, and Henri the Canuck.

The trio bent low, knowing their chances of living were slight even if they did make the wagons. Shots snapped and whined after them until finally they hit the short stretch of open field. Almost floundering, they veered sharply and sped for the nearest gap between wagons, while covering gunfire blazed from the camp.

"Drop the barricade," Fargo yelled. "We're jumping through!"

Ahead, the space between wagons was blocked by cargo, forming too high a defensive wall for the horses to scale. Behind, the gunmen were swerving in hot pursuit, sending a fusillade of avenging lead buzzing by their heads. And there was still half the clearing yet to go. Something popped like a pebble on a tight drumhead, and Henri's horse was going down, caught by a bullet.

Fargo wheeled his Ovaro so quickly that his left boot brushed the ground. He slewed in toward Henri through the crashing din of shots, calling, "My hand, grab my hand!"

As Henri's horse keeled over, Fargo shifted in the saddle and whipped the Canuck up and around behind him, almost getting brained by the old Maynard rifle that Henri had managed to hold on to. The gunmen behind them were firing more frantically, while from the camp return fire clawed savagely . . . and the blockade remained up.

"Dump that shit," Fargo shouted. "God-almighty, move it!"

Tobac was ahead, on a lathered mare that was flagging badly. Henri had squeezed in back of Fargo, hanging on by the clamp of his legs and thighs, while dexterously loading and firing with both hands. Fargo could hear the renewed rush to intercept them before they could reach shelter, now merely yards away. He could feel his Ovaro setting itself for a sliding stop to avoid crashing into both the barricade and Tobac. If that freight didn't come down . . .

But it did, crates and casks pulled hastily aside. Tobac leapt his horse over the lowered bulwark, tail-to-neck with the vaulting Ovaro. The gap, too narrow for all the bodies sailing through at the same time, swept Fargo and Henri from their awkward perch. They landed on the ground just outside, Fargo momentarily stunned by his impact with one wagon's jutting front bow. Hands dragged them to safety while others quickly rebuilt the barricade.

Despite the murderous barrage, a moment was spent acknowledging one another, a very brief reunion with surprise and relief and sorrow all tossed in. Then it was over, and the seige was on, the wagon camp ravaged by marauding gunmen.

From all directions the defenders responded lining their shots at the saffron flares that winked in the darkness outside. The corral began to reek with choking gunsmoke, now fuming so strongly that it seemed as though the wagons were burning. Lead chewed constantly into the stacked freight and through the canvas covers, zipping and ricocheting. Occasionally above the racket, Chadwick could be heard directing and exhorting while his men, rallied from the ambush and frenzied with blood lust, moved about seeking vulnerable points to invade the enclosure.

"They got one stab at us, I reckon," Carajou growled as Bridget retied the bloody bandage around his wounded arm. "God only knows when'r if the army'll wake up, but they can't risk sticking till it does. They've gotta clean us out now, fast, or pack it in."

"Speak of the devil," Bridget snapped. "Here they come."

Nearby, Fargo overheard her and gazed in the direction she was pointing. He saw that gunmen were bellying in through the grasses and across the dark bare patches, then darting for protective rocks next to the wagons. The closest gunhands were trying to shoot and run at the same time, the men behind them not overly generous with cover fire. One man, scuttling low alongside a barricade, aimed and fired at Fargo, but missed. Fargo turned, ducking reflexively, just in time to see the man paw at his belly, howling, and go down.

It had not been Carajou who'd plugged him. Fargo, glancing over his shoulder, gave Bridget an admiring grin. She had swiftly traded nursing for shooting and was again handling her pistol effectively.

But Bridget and her teamster crew could not be everywhere at once. Farther along a face peered between spokes of a wagon wheel, then an arm showed, a hand. The face, bestial in its expression of sheer ferocity, leered as the man launched out from under the wagon, springing at Bridget with a pistol in one hand, a knife in the other.

There was a snick of steel, and the man collapsed in midleap. Upwind Muldoon, armed with his butcher cleaver, had saved Bridget with a perfectly aimed toss, the cleaver splitting open the man's skull, dropping him on the spot with it buried deep inside his brain. Bridget passed Muldoon an affectionate, grateful glance. Then three gunmen came at her from under that same wagon, while more burly killers poured out from beneath some of the other wagons.

In a confused and nightmarish tangle of motion, Fargo found himself hurled back, fighting, against a wagon bed. There came a cry from Bridget; with an erupting fury he gutted one man, then whacked his rifle across an impervious face and almost bent the barrel. As the second man fell away in a spew of teeth and blood, Fargo twisted low and Bridget triggered her pistol point-blank at the third.

Teamsters, meanwhile, were desperately

scrambling to repel the onslaught. From the tilt of an ancient Conestoga, Henri the Canuck bellowed, "C'mon, you rotgut skinners! I hold no grudges and you're gonna prove it, 'cause if we ain't got Regina, we ain't got nuthin'. C'mon and show Chadwick he can't take it from real freightmen, either."

Still yelling, Henri threw himself on the nearest of the gunmen. Then Packard swiveled on his good leg and tackled another hapless Chadwick man, stabbing with one skinning knife while pulling another from his leggins. Velázquez lashed more than one eyeball out of its socket, and Enoch Welch was so intent on drawing aim that he tumbled over a wagon tongue. The entire Regina crew erupted, barflies and rogues and petty crooks, most of them wounded, but all willing to fight anyway, swinging bandaged and splinted arms, running on game legs that made them jerk with each step. Shots cracked, whips slashed, hands grappled for throats as attackers and defenders became embroiled in a brutal mess.

Tully Nickles suddenly loomed in front of Fargo. They saw each other at the same moment, Nickles raising his revolver, hatred twisting his mouth. Fargo's whole body stiffened as he thumbed back his hammer for a shot. Then he caught the hammer before it fell because Tobac happened to dart in between him and Nickles.

Tobac, glimpsing Nickles and snarling deep-throated curses, fired a wild volley that sent Nickles diving behind the corner of a wagon. A red-shirted gunman shot Tobac in the upper chest, and Tobac staggered to a halt, bent over, sagging. The red-shirted gunman's second slug was aimed at Welch, but missed when Welch staggered on a gimp knee and lurched sideward. Carajou triggered his single-barrel Damascus steel shotgun, and the red-shirted man followed Tobac down with his face blown off. Tobac didn't go clear down, though. He caught himself, straightened, holding his revolver carefully in front of him. A gunman veered within range, was nailed with lead through his kidneys, and sank to the ground sobbing hoarsely.

Fargo bounded over the bodies, hunting for Nickles or Chadwick. He raced around the corner of the wagon where Nickles had fled, only to blunder into the strewn cargo of a fallen blockade and stumbling onto one knee. That probably saved his life, a bullet clipping the air where he'd stood an instant before.

The shot had come from one of two Chadwick gunmen who were sprinting through the smoke. They were heading toward him, then Brea appeared a bit beyond, and the pair began firing at the mule skinner. Brea whirled to face them, a big Colt Dragoon jerking in his fist.

But all his skill was with a blacksnake, and he had to empty every shot from his revolver before one of these gunmen went down. The other kept right on coming, shooting. Brea staggered back, clutching at his side as a slug drilled him. He must have known how much chance he had, facing that blazing pistol with his empty iron. Yet he steadied himself and bent forward to meet the gunmen's charge, roaring defiantly in the teeth of hot lead.

Fargo was on his feet by then. He took a lunging step forward, throwing down on the gunman charging Brea. His Colt bucked, the report lost in the din of battle, but the running gunman faltered, slid to his knees, flopped over on his face.

Still clutching his side, Brea turned. When he saw Fargo standing there with the smoking revolver, a grin split his black beard and he gestured for Fargo to go on, to leave him be.

Fargo nodded, but found it hard to return the grin.

Then, on past Brea, Fargo glimpsed Nickles and Chadwick.

11

Tully Nickles and Luther Chadwick were tenacious men.

Both had worked doggedly to stop the Regina shipment, Chadwick because he was greedy to take over, Nickles because he was hired to do the job. And neither was a slouch at fighting, not shirking safely behind the lines, but mixing into it, head, ears, and feet, determined to win. As Fargo eyed them, though, he thought they must now be pretty desperate to destroy the outfit, what with time running against them and the need to conceal their tracks. Desperate enough so that if they couldn't smash the train, they'd burn it up.

The Morgan Fargo had seen Chadwick ride stood nervously by a wagon about a quarter of the way around the circle. And stooping to light a pile of brush that laid against the wagon wheel was Chadwick. Nickles stood to one side, holding an empty bucket, the typical grease bucket that hung on the tailgate of every wagon, filled with a mixture of resin, tar, and tallow that the teamsters used to lubricate the axles. The goop didn't burn well unless a hot fire, such as the brush would cause, got it really cooking, and then it'd just keep on burning, hell to put out. The resultant blaze would certainly incinerate the dry old wagons and their cargo right down to the wheel rims.

Fargo sprinted toward them as swiftly yet as quietly as he could, hoping not to forewarn them. They wouldn't pot-shoot at him, like a couple of rumdum mule skinners unable to hit a mule at three paces with a scattergun. Nickles made his living by his skill with a gun. And Chadwick, according to all the scuttlebutt, had always won before.

Flame writhed up the side of the wagon. Chadwick straightened, and Fargo sped faster, bringing his revolver to bear on Chadwick's spine, thumbing the hammer and feeling no guilt about shooting this lowlife in the back. As if Chadwick sensed someone coming, he suddenly spun, spotted Fargo, and ducked around the wagon. Fargo's bullet seared a line across the shoulder of his jacket and burrowed harmlessly into the wooden sideboard of the next wagon.

Chadwick was gone, but Nickles was not. He pivoted, triggering as he was turning, lead plowing into wood and earth in pursuit of Fargo with the hasty aim of a shootist caught unaware.

Immediately Fargo sighted and squeezed. There was no shot, no discharge, the hammer falling on an empty chamber or a defective load. Having kept count, he knew the revolver wasn't empty. He also knew a bum load could jam the action just enough, that firing the next round might cause the revolver to blow back like a bomb in his face.

Nickles may not have realized why, but he sure knew that Fargo wasn't shooting. "Hah, you're my meat. You're history."

Slugs from his pistol snapped in the air like fangs closing about Fargo. He flung himself at a headlong angle beneath the nearest wagon, cursing silently as he began switching the revolver's cylinder for a loaded one from his pocket. He heard the tromping of boots on the other side of the wagon, and then Chadwick's conceited voice, "If the piss-ant shows over here, Tully, I'll seive him."

"Leave him be, Mist' Chadwick, I've divvies on him," Nickles bawled peevishly. Kneeling, he fired twice under the wagon at Fargo.

Fargo rolled, slithering to avoid being hit while frantically trying to finish reloading. Nickles triggered again and looked very startled when his pistol failed to fire. Fargo almost burst out laughing as Nickles clicked off three more empty rounds in rapid succession, then scrambled to his feet and backed hurriedly to reload.

Tightening the cylinder pin and closing the loading lever, Fargo was ready to hunt the hunter. Quickly he slid from the wagon and out by the tongue, spotting Nickles easily in the flickery light of the budding fire. As though going to fetch more ammunition, the redhead trotted away while emptying spent cartridges one by one—a tempting target, but at a poor angle. Fargo checked his impatience and began to run only to lose him in darkness and gunsmoke.

Nickles had vanished only temporarily, Fargo felt sure. But before he materialized again, Bridget appeared from between the two wagons ahead. She was in a rush, evidently alarmed and horrified by the fire. She never saw Nickles rise out of nowhere, stalking her.

Fargo saw Nickles and tore ito a mad run. "Behind you!"

She heard Fargo and wheeled. Nickles loomed over her, hands clutching. Bridget backpedaled and drew her .36 revolver. She fired, but Nickles spoiled her aim with a lunging, long-armed slap to her gun wrist, and her shot whistled by him. Before she could fire again, he seized her arm and twisted her around.

With Bridget now thrust between him and Nickles, Fargo didn't dare risk using his weapons. Yet making Bridget his shield was not Nickles' intention; he wanted her pistol. Frantically he groped and mauled her, wrenching her about as she resisted gamely, struggling in his frenzied grip.

Fargo reached Nickles just as he was swinging Bridget from her feet. Fargo's hand bit into the deep muscle crowning the ridge of Nickles' shoulder—a cruel, implacable bite of fingers, crippling in their savagery. Nickles freed Bridget and looped a left-fisted roundhouse at Fargo. Fargo turned a half-pace sideways, ducking the blow. Bridget was careless for an instant, her attention briefly drawn by the punch at Fargo. Nickles' right hand squirreled around, swept out, and snatched the pistol away from her palm. Then he launched into a wild backward run to gain space, leveling the pistol at Fargo.

Bridget screamed, "Down! Down, Skye, quick!"

Fargo would not go down. Instead, he took Bridget high on the arm with his left hand and forced her downward, while with his right he whipped up his revolver.

Nickles fired, and if he felt anything about killing these two, it would have been joy. His shot occurred almost simultaneously with Fargo's gunshot, but Fargo's bullet was already buried in Nickles' heart when the redhead pulled the trigger, so Nickles' shot went wide, whining off into the air. Nickles stepped back, dead, a half-pace, and Fargo nailed him with a second and third shot as insurance. Nickles went down as though he were boneless, collapsing on the ground faceup, one arm stretched out, with Bridget's pistol lying in his open palm like a gift.

"Thanks," Bridget said shakily. "I . . . Lord, the fire!"

The blaze was licking up the side of the wagon now, and Fargo knew once it reached the canvas there'd be no stopping it. With Bridget hustling alongside, he headed toward the burning Conestoga.

On the way, he kept a sharp lookout for Chadwick. He saw no sign of the Consolidated owner, but in scanning the field and the tumultuous brawl of fighters, it seemed to him that the Regina crew was gaining the advantage. The gunmen were edging back, not quite retreating but no longer attacking—stalled, scattered, by mule skinners contemptuous of death, resigned to it, in fact.

"Up an at 'em, cuss you," Fargo heard Henri raving. "We're a batch of yaller dogs who wouldn't know guts if they were thrown in our face, but we're going to skin these rabbits if I have to peel 'em all myself! Afterward, *mes amis* the drinks are on Capt'n Fargo."

"For long as Colonel Garabedian's shine lasts, anyway," Fargo muttered, chuckling under his breath.

Reaching the fire, he and Bridget tossed dirt on the flames, then he tore off his shirt and beat at them. He stretched and ripped a piece of canvas from the hoops before it could catch on fire. His hands were burned and his chest was blistered when they finally realized the fire was out. Bridget wanted to smear some axle grease on his burns, but he refused, fearing a slippery grip on his gun could cost him his life.

Suddenly Carajou let out a hoarse shout. His huge hand was pointing toward the northeast, where a billowy cloud of dust or smoke seemed to be smudging the sky. There was an odd faltering to the conflict as teamster and gunman alike stared querulously at it.

"Recognize 'em?" Henri called.

Carajou peered, then replied authoritatively, "Buffalo."

Dimly from afar sounded the ratty blat of a bugle.

"Buffalo," Velázquez hooted. "*Cretino,* those're troopers."

The reaction was immediate. Gunmen raced for their horses out around the fringe of the camp, vaulting onto the saddle and fleeing toward the surrounding woods. Fargo had been watching for Chadwick, and now for the first time since the fire, he saw the man making a frantic dash for his

Morgan. With a flinty smile at Bridget, Fargo took off after Chadwick at a dead run.

Glimpsing Fargo as he was mounting, Chadwick hit saddle and wheeled to face him. A slug scraped hotly across Fargo's cheek. He steadied himself just in time to see Chadwick spur his horse forward. The enraged man bent far over, carbine thrust out, firing as he came. Another bullet nipped Fargo. He refused to give ground, taking aim as he ran. The Morgan thundered past, so close that Fargo had to dodge aside. Chadwick triggered again, and Fargo felt the lead clip his sleeve, then he shot the horse in the chest.

The Morgan staggered for a few more yards and then plunged. In a stunning display of horsemanship, Chadwick gauged his horse's last moments, throwing himself clear by rolling back over the falling animal's rump. The dust formed a shield around them for an instant, and when it dissipated, Chadwick was tearing riverward without his carbine.

Fargo sped on in pursuit.

Chadwick raged obscenely at Fargo, opening fire with his shoulder-holstered pistol. But Fargo came charging on, the notion of Chadwick's escape making his flesh feel cold and grainy. Then Chadwick turned and launched upriver along the bank, which proved to be a muddy struggle through prickly grasses and interwoven plants that flourished along with swarms of gnats in the brackish shoals.

Fargo hit the bank, slid, and almost fell to his knees. He continued on, seeing Chadwick wading and stumbling a short distance ahead. He was impatient to catch up, but he was as hampered as

Chadwick by the muck. Chadwick, turning, fired and slipped from the recoil, but forced Fargo to dive, the man's offhand shooting accurate enough to send a bullet grazing his beard.

In the clearing behind Fargo, Colonel Garabedian rode at the head of a column of bluebellies. As he lay flat, craning his head around, Fargo could see the formation wheeling after the gunmen, who were beating a retreat as fast as they could gallop. Many found themselves boxed in and threw down their weapons. Some made a fight of it, knowing the gallows was their only future. A few crashed into the timber and could be heard thrashing through the underbrush, bending under low branches, while behind them charged troopers following their readily traceable paths through the woodlands.

Chadwick started scuttling up the bank, clawing for the top. Fargo loosed a shot, which missed Chadwick but brought him down anyway. The upper portion of the bank was a steep and exposed climb, and Chadwick, sensing he'd never get up there before Fargo got him, dipped into a watery thatch of cattails behind an earthen mound.

Fargo, flat on his belly in the mud, knew he was an open target, as Chadwick stuck his Starr .44 revolver out of the cattails and triggered from behind the mound. The hard, deadly crack of heavy-caliber timbre bounced echoing off the bank. Mud sprayed Fargo's face, and he swiped at his eyes with his sleeve, figuring, What the hell, no use lying here and dying.

He rose to one knee, and a slug plucked at his pant leg. Then he was vaulting forward again, hunching low, training his revolver on those cat-tails. Chadwick leaned and inched a bit higher to get in another, better-aimed shot, but Fargo kept on sprinting as he snap-shot into the reeds. Chadwick groaned, and Fargo could hear flopping and threshings in the water as though someone had hooked a big fish in the shallows.

Fargo plunged to his belly again at the edge of the mound and crawled cautiously forward to the cattail thicket. Scattered gunfire still burst from around the wagon camp, but it all seemed far-away, in some other world. In his world there was only himself and Chadwick and a small pool of brackish water between them. He eased nearer, holstering his revolver and snaking out his hunting knife.

Chadwick was on his side, his chin turned and dragging in the plant-thick water, one hand holding his Starr straight out and level with Fargo's face. Fargo stabbed out, slashing while he rolled wildly to one side, the .44 blasting in his ears. Chadwick squirmed and coughed, then rolled over and triggered a bullet, drilling into the water near Fargo's left ear. Still grunting and muttering curses, Chadwick tried to lift his revolver up to a level with Fargo's head, his hand faltering, the gun tilting.

Fargo dragged himself within a foot of Chad-wick's face. The eyes were sunken and invisible, and under the mouth the water was darker, the darkest color of all. Chadwick coughed and sagged a little, trying to keep his chin up high, his mouth and nose from sinking down too far into the drink. And all the while he was concentrating on his pis-tol, trying to raise it that necessary bit.

A hard man to kill, Fargo thought, but I'm getting there.

Chadwick's mouth opened and red froth bubbled. "You're a fuckin' turd, and I'll deball you yet."

Fargo reached out and pushed Chadwick's face under the water. Chadwick didn't have enough strength to struggle at all.

Leaving Chadwick there facedown, Fargo climbed the bank. He could hear the gun fray tapering to a few erratic shots and screams, and could smell the aftermath of powder smoke drifting over the area as he started back toward the camp. A riderless horse galloped past him, red foam drooling from its mouth, its eyes crazed and rolling.

When Fargo arrived, dawn was beginning to ooze across the eastern horizon. The shooting had all died away, and there was no more fighting, no more resistance, the soldiers now disarming the surrendering gunmen. Another detail of troopers was burying the dead, while others with Upwind Muldoon were handling the wounded. Fargo spotted Brea, still holding his side, his hand blood-soaked. Several others were around him, already patched and resting.

After a moment, Fargo located Bridget conversing with Colonel Garabedian. Bridget asked, "Are you all right, Skye?"

To which the colonel gave a snort, chiming in, "O' course he's okay. But what happened to Luther Chadwick? I understand you ran off with him, eh?"

Fargo smiled lightly. "Oh, back aways. He's going nowhere."

"That's good. I'd hate for Chadwick to skip out on his own party. Miz Delahay was explainin' he threw quite a blast, especially at first, and I'm here to tell you it was more'n a man could sleep through. Such a commotion and huckety-buck!" Garabedian grinned, glancing at Enoch Welch limping toward them, then he eyed Fargo again. "I'm told your boys had Chadwick's mob fairly routed by the time we wandered in. Well, I'm just glad you held 'em off as long as you did."

"I'm kind of glad myself," Fargo said, and turned to see what Welch wanted. Before Welch could say, a strange, scuffling noise arose faintly from the direction of the trail. Momentarily two men could be seen, badly wounded, carrying the body of a third while staggering along the trail. These three were all that was left of the teamsters who'd stayed out at the draw. And the man in the middle was Tiny Quinelle; his head lolled and one arm dangled uselessly, but he was gesturing defiantly with the other. Even at this distance, they could hear the big man bellowing and bellyaching, "If'n you drop me again, God help you, because you'll need it—when I get well!"

"Alive! Well, we might've known," Welch said happily. "The devil wouldn't have him, and spit him back. Say, Capt'n, we figure we'll have the outfit in rollin' condition in about three hours."

Fargo nodded. "Push it along," he said quietly.

"I think we better get this load straight to the post then, get it delivered, and signed off before anything more can happen," Garabedian suggested as he slowly surveyed the carnage. "By rights, by all the odds, it shouldn't've ended this way. You shouldn't've ended on top. Beats the hell out of me how you did it."

"Me?" Fargo protested. "Not me. My crew did it all."

"Sure. A pack of scapegrace derelicts, they did it. Uh-huh." Colonel Garabedian sighed and bit off the end of a cigar. "One of these days, Mist' Fargo, you're going to kill off everyone fit to kill off. Then where'll you be? The only thing left will be to bite yourself and commit suicide."

LOOKING FORWARD!

**The following is the opening
section from the next novel in the exciting
Trailsman series from Signet:**

THE TRAILSMAN #59
THUNDER HAWK

*Wyoming, 1860, an untamed land
where the good and evil in men's souls
come together as surely as the waters
of the Wind River and the Bighorn meet. . . .*

On a warm summer afternoon it began.

That was the start of it. And the end, too, most everyone said.

But they were wrong.

It began as silent and fierce as the red-tailed hawk's dive, with a strike so swift its prey hardly has time to cry out. On a warm summer afternoon, just south of the Bighorn mountains, five wagons rolled northward. Four were big Conestogas with reinforced hickory axles and one an Owensboro Seed bed wagon carrying extra water casks, tools and supplies. The wagon train had started in Utah, its destination the rich farming land of

Montana territory. It was perhaps one of the grim twists of fate that it was not a larger, stronger wagon train, but three wagons never arrived to join. Yet Hiram Dodd, the wagonmaster, decided to go on, anyway. Dreams are impatient travelers.

Like all those who braved the untamed, uncharted land, each had come for their own reasons. Each carried his own baggage of hope, the wagon train a symbol of a new life. But to the near-naked, bronze-skinned horsemen unseen in the thickness of the boxelder, the wagon train was another kind of symbol. It was the mark of the intruder, of those who came to rule, to command, to own the land when the land was no one's to own. Worst of all, they cloaked themselves in fine words but left a trail of broken promises. Like the weeds that threatened to choke a pond, they had to be cut down.

The tall warrior with the intense, black-coal eyes wore a hawk's beak pendant around his neck. When he raised his arm and brought it down in a short, chopping motion, the cry of the Cheyenne sounded in the warm, summer afternoon. Their attack was as perfectly executed as it was fierce. They came in waves of galloping ponies, each wave firing arrows in alternate volleys. In seconds, the blue sky was almost invisible through the flying shafts that seemed to go on endlessly.

The wagons were never able to form a circle, unable to halt and unable to flee. The attack was merciful only because it was over so quickly. On a warm, summer afternoon—an attack on a wagon train, like so many that had come before and since.

But that was five years back.

Since then, there had been five years of warm summer afternoons. That particular afternoon was but a footnote in the history of broken dreams.

And now it had been born again.

Not that the big man with the lake-blue eyes knew it, not yet. All he knew was a sense of disbelief that was fast spiraling into anger inside him and he peered hard at the man that faced him from the other side of the old desk. "You're damn right I don't understand it, Will Conklin," Skye Fargo said. "You send for me to ride trail for you and now you say you can't take me on?"

The rancher's normally relaxed face struggled uncomfortably and his fingers nervously turned a keychain. "I'll pay for your traveling time here, Fargo," he said. "I can't do more'n that."

"Hell, Will, you know I don't care about that," Fargo snapped. "I can go to Jack Tisdale. He's always wanted me to break trail for him."

"He won't take you on, either," the rancher said. "Not now."

Fargo felt the frown digging deeper into his brow. "What'the hell is this all about, Will?" he rasped.

"It's about Bertram Thorgard. He wants to see you and he got the word to us," the rancher said, his lips pulling back in distaste.

"Who the hell's Bertram Thorgard?" Fargo blurted.

"Bertram Thorgard is a lot of money and a lot of power," Will Conklin said.

"He own you? Jack Tisdale, too?" Fargo demanded.

"No, but he owns the bank and the bank holds notes from every rancher around here. That includes me and Jack. Word came down that we hire you and the bank calls in our notes," the rancher said.

"Son of a bitch," Fargo grunted.

"Just what I said," Will agreed. "But I can't have my notes called up, now. Neither can Jack or any of the others. I don't know the man, never met him and he's got my hands tied."

"Why the hell didn't he just send word for me to come see him?" Fargo asked himself as much as Will Conklin.

"Bertram Thorgard does things his own way, I hear," the rancher said.

Fargo's eyes flared blue ice. "I don't much like his way," he growled.

"Don't blame you, old friend. But he does want you. I'd pay the man a visit," Will said. "His place is north of Shadyville up past the Sweetwater."

Fargo let himself frown into space for a moment as his thoughts leapfrogged. "Only two reasons I'll pay him a visit," he growled finally. "One, Vivian Keeler's got a place in Shadyville and I've been promising to visit her for two years, and two, to tell Mister Bertram Thorgard it's not smart to try to lean on me."

"I imagine you'll do that real well," Will Conklin said, coming around the desk to put his hand on the big man's shoulder. "I'm sorry, I didn't want to go along with him. I just couldn't help it."

Fargo's chiseled face relaxed and a smile came to his lips. "I understand, Will. Pay off that note and be a free man again," he said.

"Quick as I can, that's for sure," the rancher said and with a handshake, Fargo strode out of the house to where his horse waited beside the hitching post. The magnificent Ovaro seemed to shine in the afternoon sun, the jet black fore-and-hind-quarters gleaming, the midsection pure white. Fargo swung into the saddle and turned the horse northward across the Wyoming territory. He rode hard, anger still inside him. The colossal nerve of Bertram Thorgard defied belief. He was plainly an arrogant man with the power of his money and willing to use that power any way he could. Men such as Bertram Thorgard came to believe the world and everyone in it was made for them. He would have to be told differently, Fargo grunted as he crested a long hill and started down the other side.

His eyes scanned the land as he rode, the habit as much a part of him as his skin. This was redman's land. The Arapaho rode here, and sometimes the Assiniboin ventured down from the north as did the Sioux. But mostly this was Cheyenne land and it was easy to understand why the Indian fought so savagely for this countryside. The Wyoming territory provided both forest and plains and every kind of game for every kind of need; buffalo and antelope, deer and jackrabbit on the plains; moose, elk, bear in the forests; game for food and hides, for furs and robes and plenty of badger, otter and beaver for small pelts. But for all its richness, it was a fierce land where winters came on killing winds. Yet the land provided for those who knew how to meet it on its own terms.

It was a land where trial and hardship could bring out the best in men's souls. And where the opportunities for unbridled greed and power could bring out the worst, Fargo added grimly and immediately thought of Bertram Thorgard. But he pushed the man's name aside and let his mind turn to more pleasant things as he rode alongside a deep stand of dark green Balsam. Vivian would be well worth the trip. He smiled and memories rushed at him—remembrances of warm, eager lips, of clasping legs that were smooth tentacles of desire. But mostly he remembered a woman wise enough to understand her own needs and strong enough to abide by them. Vivian had married her husband because he needed a woman to do a woman's work and she needed a provider. There had been an understanding, an arrangement—and loving was never part of it. When he died, she'd carried on to find a new life for herself at another time with other needs.

In between, Fargo smiled again, he'd met her and it had been good, real good. Vivian was a woman you could respect out of bed as much as you could enjoy her in bed, and that wasn't easy to find. The smile still edged his lips as he saw the long shadows marching down the rolling hillsides. A salesman with a glass-windowed delivery wagon hung with pots and pans came into view along a road and Fargo sent the Ovaro across his path.

"The Sweetwater's dead ahead of you, Mister," the man said in answer to Skye's question. "And Shadyville's straight on."

"The Thorgard place," Fargo asked.

"You can get there without going through Shadyville," the man said. "Take a left soon as you cross the Sweetwater. Follow a thin line of Yellow Poplar. It'll lead you right to his spread."

Fargo nodded thanks and sent the pinto into a canter until he came to the narrow river, found a sandbar that afforded easy crossing and rode to the other bank. He spotted the long, thin line of trees at once and followed their path to reach a large ranch as dusk began to settle across the land. He rode past neat, well-kept posthole fencing to arrive at a large house, the bottom fieldstone, the top gold oak shingle, with two chimneys and a gabled window at one side of the roof. A rich man's house, he decided as he halted at the front door, dismounted and left the Ovaro at a brass-topped hitching rail. Two large stables took shape behind the main house and he glimpsed ranch-hands at their chores. The front door of the house opened as he reached it and he faced the man whose bulk loomed in the doorway.

"You're Fargo," the man said in a voice that resonated with authority. He was a big man with a heavy face, hair still black though the man looked to be in his fifties. His face had disdain in its every line—the jutting jaw, the cold blue eyes, the wide mouth that turned down at the corners.

"Good guess," Fargo said.

"No guess. I was given a good description of you. I'm Bertram Thorgard," the man said.

"I know," Fargo said.

The man's thick brows arched. "You were given a description of me?" he ventured.

"Let's say you fit what I expected," Fargo said.

"What's that?" Bertram Thorgard asked.

"Somebody who needs trimming down to size," Fargo snapped.

The man's smile was one of tolerant amusement. "I expected a certain amount of resentment," he said smoothly.

"You got it," Fargo growled.

"Please come inside," the man said and Fargo followed him into a huge living room furnished with heavy, mahogany furniture, rich maroon drapes framing the windows and tapestries on the walls. It was a quietly opulent room that fitted Bertram Thorgard comfortably.

"You've a brass pot full of nerve, Thorgard. What makes you think you can maneuver folks around to suit yourself?" Fargo frowned.

"You're here, aren't you?" Thorgard said diffidently.

Fargo felt himself flare at the smug truth in the man's answer. "For my own reasons, not yours," he flung back.

"Reasons don't interest me. Results do," Bertram Thorgard said. The man was not easily ruffled, Fargo conceded inwardly.

"Why didn't you send word to me you wanted to talk? Why all this beating around the bush?" Fargo threw at the man's calm disdain.

"I was ready for you when I heard Conklin had sent for you. I wanted you now, not later, after you'd finished with him. Besides, I wanted you to have reason to listen to me," Thorgard answered. "You must at least be curious."

"Talk fast. I don't listen long," Fargo said, ignoring the question and the truth it contained.

"I've two thousand dollars for you, Fargo. That is a lot of money," Thorgard said.

Fargo felt his brows arch. "A powerful lot of money," he agreed.

"I'm going to bring my grandson back to me. I need you for that," the man said, his heavy face darkening suddenly and an urgency coming into his voice.

"Why?" Fargo asked, his eyes narrowing.

"To find him, first. Then to take him," the man said. "The Cheyenne have him."

"They take him in a wagon train attack?" Fargo asked.

"Yes, and now I'm ready to take him back," Thorgard said.

"Just like that. Just walk in and take him back," Fargo remarked, sarcasm thick in his voice.

"No, not just like that. I know how hard it will be," Thorgard said and leaned forward, his heavy face growing more massive. "But I've planned out every part of it. For three years I've prepared, and now I've put it all into action. I've used all the power of connections and money, I've picked my men, arranged details, laid out plans for escape and pursuit. I can't fail. All I need is you, the Trailsman, the very best, to find that red devil that has my grandson."

"There are a hell of a lot of Cheyenne," Fargo said.

"I know that. That's why I need you, to find the right one," Thorgard said.

"How old is the boy?" Fargo asked.

"Four," the man said.

"It'll be like looking for a needle in a haystack. Lots of kids are taken in wagon train attacks," Fargo said.

"There are things to help you. His mother was also taken in the attack, a very blond young woman and I know exactly when and where the attack took place," Thorgard said.

"How do you know that?" Fargo queried.

"A man who reached the scene an hour after the attack," Thorgard said.

Fargo fastened Thorgard with a probing stare. "Even if I could find the boy, what then? You still think you can walk into a Cheyenne camp and take him?"

"I'll show you how we take the boy and escape. I've a blueprint for every step of it," Thorgard said.

Fargo let a wry sound escape his lips. "You've a blueprint for suicide," he said. "Don't include me in it."

"I need you. You're the only one that can track down the Cheyenne who has the boy," the man shouted. "You're the key to all the rest of it."

"Find another key," Fargo said, and turning, strode from the room. He pulled the door open, stepped outside and felt the big man's frame at his heels.

"I'll double the money. Four thousand," Thorgard shouted.

Fargo continued walking to the Ovaro. "I've still only got one neck. I want to hang onto it a spell longer," he tossed back. "I'm out. Don't bother me anymore."

"No, you're in, Fargo," the man returned.

Fargo swung onto the Ovaro and paused to frown back at the man. "You really don't understand, do you?" he said. "Forget it. Find somebody else."

"I don't take no for an answer, Fargo. I get what I want and I want you. I need you to find the boy," Thorgard boomed. "You're in. You'll be back."

"Hell I will," Fargo snapped and sent the pinto into a canter. But he felt the frown dig into his forehead again as he rode. He wanted to dismiss the man as nothing more than an arrogant braggart, used to taking or buying whatever he wanted and now shouting empty words to take away the sting of defeat. But he knew better. Bertram Thorgard wasn't the kind for empty words. Underneath his arrogance was something else—a terrible darkness that gave his disdain an icy, searing edge.

But the man had no hold on him, Fargo reminded himself, none at all and he wondered why he felt strangely uncomfortable as he rode through the dusk.